THE MAGICAL STORM II

THE MAGICAL STORM II

"THE LAST MAMMOTHS"

Written and Illustrated by:

John Stiles Smith

ISBN: 979-8-218-60042-6

CONTENTS

INTRODUCTION

We know how bad a virus can be. Our shared experiences from the COVID-19 pandemic in 2020 showed us how true that statement unfolded. *The Magical Storm II: The Last Mammoths* was originally written in 2017 and copyrighted as a screenplay in 2018. This is a story about extinction, and in 2020 we learned how vulnerable even humanity can be. Much like our characters—JJ, Calvin, and Brad—who must work together to face challenges to succeed and achieve a positive outcome, we, as members of humanity, must also come together and collaborate for our survival. The boys must carry out their destiny with *The Magical Storm, making a difference one storm at a time.*

Chapter One

THE GAME

A loud *pop* fills the air as a fastball slams into a catcher's mitt. Dust flies off the mitt, and within a split second, the call is heard.

"Strike two!" an umpire yells out.

The crowd lets out a collective groan. The atmosphere is tense, and chatter fills the park. Stepping away from the plate is second baseman Brad Thompson, who had pitched a shutout until he was pulled in the top of the seventh due to league pitching regulations. A series of errors by the home team and some timely hitting by the visitors have made for an exciting baseball game, but now the season is on the line. Brad taps his shoes with his bat and knocks some dirt loose as he glances out toward center field and checks out the scoreboard that reads,

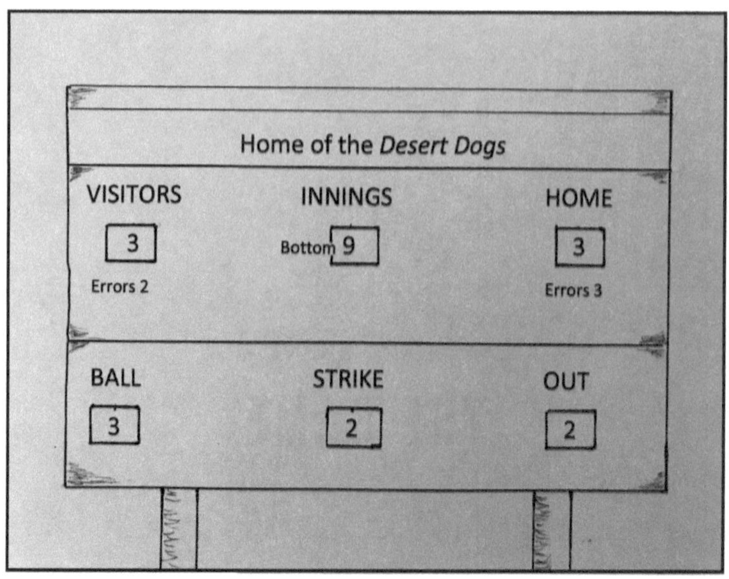

Below the scoreboard on the outfield fence lined with local business sponsors is a sign that reads, "Middle School Regional Baseball Championship."

Brad knows the opposing team doesn't want to intentionally walk the winning run, which would be him. What the other team doesn't know is that the defensive changes his coach made in the seventh inning involve good infielders but not good hitters. So, if they go into extra innings, Brad's team will face the top of the opponent's lineup and their best offensive opportunity. Therefore, for Brad, it's now or never.

The pitcher and Brad make eye contact. It's a brief stare down as Brad steps into the left batter's box. Suddenly, in the background, his friends, JJ, Calvin, along with JJ's sister

Amy, and her friend Cindi can be heard cheering Brad on. The boys are wearing their usual attire, Calvin in his khakis, and always with his backpack, but JJ has something new: a red bandana wrap around his cowboy hat with the word 'Inka.' She was the young Hopi princess that JJ met during his first journey with the Magical Storm and a reminder of his fond memories of their adventure together.

"Pick out a good one!" JJ calls out.

"Yeah, number nine, protect the plate!" Calvin adds.

"Just hit the ball, weirdo!" Amy yells out.

Brad takes a quick peek toward the stands, knowing Amy is watching. He looks up and smiles as he sees Amy rolling her eyes. Then he flashes a serious, determined look and gets set for the pitch. Brad looks ready, expecting another fastball.

Out on the mound, the pitcher gets set, then steps off the rubber and looks toward his third baseman. They exchange subtle nods, possibly indicating an inside pitch. With the clue given, he resumes his pre-pitch stance on the mound and smoothly gets into his windup. After a pretty good pitch motion from a thirteen-year-old, the ball zips toward the plate.

Brad is set, and his facial expression, along with his eyes, tells you it's a pitch he likes. Brad takes a swing, and the *crack* of the bat can be heard as the ball blasts off. Brad makes good contact but drills a line drive foul ball over the home team's dugout.

The ball bounces past JJ and Calvin, ricochets off the bench, and rolls down the footboard of the bleachers. Suddenly, a mad rush of about a dozen young kids stampede past JJ and Calvin, prompting Calvin to give them a precarious look.

"What's the deal?" a puzzled Calvin asks as JJ shrugs and smiles, keeping his eyes on the game.

"Yeah, it's baseball," JJ responds. "Pick out a good one, Brad!" he calls out, cheering his buddy on.

Back at the plate, Brad gets set with fixed eyes, ready for the next pitch. Within a second Brad's eyes widened as he sees the pitch he was looking for: a fastball, knee-high and right down the center of the plate. Then suddenly, without hesitation, Brad takes a mighty swing, and the loud *crack* of the bat launches the ball like a missile out toward center field.

The ball sails high and to the deepest part of center field. As it travels through the air, the center fielder breaks back on the ball, keeping his eyes focused on the prize. To his right, the left fielder runs towards center field to serve as backup on the play.

Meanwhile, back in the infield, Brad is racing toward second base with no intention of stopping. In the background, in the seats, the crowd is going wild. Amy and her friend are jumping wildly, while JJ and Calvin watch with much anticipation. JJ sports a curious expression, as he has a slight idea what Brad may be up to.

Out in center field, the center fielder is hustling to catch the deep fly ball. Then something crazy happens. As the ball is coming down past the center fielder, it smacks the top of the fence but hits a bracket that connects two pipes of the fence. The ball suddenly takes a wild forty-five-degree ricochet off the fence and bounces out toward left-center, behind the left fielder, who is racing toward center field. Simultaneously, the center fielder crashes into the fence and tumbles to the ground helplessly out of the play. With the left fielder seeing the ball behind him, he slams on the brakes and quickly turns around, dashing toward the loose ball.

The third base coach, one of Brad's teammates, sees the left fielder closing in on the ball and puts his arms up, waving for Brad to stop at third base. But Brad is having no thoughts of stopping; he sees his opportunity and puts a slight arc in his running path to hit third base at full throttle. Brad's baseball helmet falls off as he charges toward third with his cleats tearing up a dirt trail.

Out in left field, the outfielder picks the ball up and fires it to the shortstop, who is ready for the relay and quickly throws it to the catcher, who is in position at home plate as the umpire gets ready for the call.

Up in the bleachers, the home team crowd is going wild as Brad pounds third base in his race to the plate. JJ sports a smile as he cheers his buddy on.

"All the way, Brad!" JJ yells out. Calvin looks a bit skeptical and gives JJ a puzzled glance.

"Man, I can't believe he's going to try this!" a surprised

Calvin says as JJ flashes a grin. Amy and her friend continue to jump up and down with double overhead fist bumps.

"Can you run any faster, weirdo?" she calls out.

Back in the infield, Brad is making his final dash toward the plate as the shortstop fires the ball to the catcher, and the umpire readies himself for the call. The action is fast and tense as Brad streaks down the final ten feet to the plate. Suddenly, Brad breaks into his slide as the ball rips toward the awaiting catcher. Then almost simultaneously, the ball is caught by the catcher as Brad's baseball shoe plows through the dirt inches away from home plate. But the throw is slightly high, and Brad appears to have slid under the tag. Dust fills the air, and the crowd is silent in anticipation, along with both dugouts. All eyes are on the umpire when, within a split second, he extends both arms out with palms down.

"Safe!" the home plate umpire yells out as Brad fist-bumps and flashes a big smile. Within a second or two, pandemonium breaks out inside the Desert Dog's dugout. Brad's teammates rush the field and swarm their hero. With collective team effort, Brad is hoisted overhead and, as if made for a movie, is carried off the field to wild, loud cheers and applause from the home team fans.

As Brad enjoys the jubilation, he scans the bleachers,

looking for his friends, and within a moment, they catch eyes. Then Brad grabs his elbows and conducts an up and down motion, briefly stopping to point forward. He repeats the pattern a couple more times before getting carried away.

In the bleachers, JJ, Calvin, and Amy are still applauding Brad's momentous effort when JJ flashes a puzzled expression.

"What's he doing?" JJ asks curiously. Calvin smiles and nods.

"He's telling us to meet at the park," Calvin responds as JJ smiles and gets Brad's gesture.

"Great! Then let's go!" JJ announces as he leads the way down the stairs.

Several minutes later, outside the baseball field, JJ, Calvin, Amy, and her friend gather before the boys go to meet Brad. But Amy and her friend have other plans, as she reminds JJ.

"Mom said I could go to Cindi's house for an hour after the game," Amy informs. JJ nods.

"Sure, but have them drop you off at the park. Mom's going to be busy for a couple of hours, and you're supposed to hang with me," JJ says as Amy gives her brother a sneer with a head tilt.

"Oh well, doesn't that sound like fun," Amy sarcastically responds. "Later!" With that, Amy and Cindi walk away, while JJ and Calvin head toward the local park for their rendezvous with Brad.

Chapter Two

THE STORM

About an hour later, the three boys walk toward a swing set at the park. In the background, a slide, monkey bars, a merry-go-round, and up a slight incline to a basketball court where three boys are playing some hoops. Calvin pushes his glasses off his nose and looks at his two friends.

"So, by the way, what's with everybody getting so crazy over a foul ball hit into the stands?" a curious Calvin asks. Brad abruptly stops and flashes an astonished look on his face at the question.

"What?" a puzzled Brad responds. "A foul ball!"

Calvin and JJ share a glance, then Calvin looks at Brad.

"Yeah, like, what's the deal with a foul ball?" Calvin questions. Brad rears his head back and gives Calvin the "look."

"Let me tell you," Brad starts. "Catching a foul ball is

like…an instant surprise party with gifts and memories that will last forever. Dude, you're not only at the game, but now you've become part of that game for the rest of your life. Something one day you can tell your grandkids about," Brad concludes. Calvin and JJ share a surprised look.

"I never knew he had it in him," Calvin mutters to JJ, who shrugs and flashes a grin.

"Well, you just never know," JJ responds with a chuckle as the boys continue their walk to the park. Brad suddenly stops as he looks toward the ground.

"Hey, look, some rope!" Brad says as he points to a pile of rope on the ground. He picks it up and tosses it to JJ.

JJ grabs the rope and, without hesitation, starts to make a small loop knot at one of the ends. Calvin and Brad intently watch JJ as they find themselves a seat on the swing set. In no time JJ starts to twirl a lariat loop from left to right. Soon, he has the loop moving in fluid, rhythmic motions when suddenly, he hops through the large loop and gracefully steps over the rope as it moves left to right. Calvin and Brad rear their heads back with wide eyes as they watch JJ's impressive moves. Then Brad, always the comedian, quickly jumps off the swing set seat and starts slapping his thigh as he pounds his gym shoe up and down off the ground.

"Howdy, partners, here we go…Hoop de do, oh, hoop de da," Brad sings as he continues to pound his thigh and stomp his foot. Suddenly, JJ spins the large loop over his head and whips it toward Brad. Within a split second, JJ has lassoed Brad with both arms to his side as he flashes a dumbfounded expression. JJ gives Brad a smile and a nod, while Calvin is cracking up.

"Nifty," Calvin says with chuckle. "Oh, hoop de do, oh, hoop de da," he sings as he mocks Brad. The boys share a laugh as Brad tosses the rope to the side.

"Man, he got you good…So what's next?" Calvin asks as a basketball unexpectedly rolls up next to them.

"Well, we can play some basketball," Brad replies as he picks up the basketball. "But first, let me show you nifty." JJ and Calvin share a curious glance, then watch what Brad is up to. Without missing a beat, Brad starts to spin the basketball on his middle finger. Calmly, he takes the basketball while it's still spinning behind his back. He gives JJ and Calvin a half grin as he brings the spinning ball around his back to his front side on the middle finger of the other hand. JJ and Calvin, impressed, share a smile and a nod.

"So, is Amy on her way?" Brad asks. Abruptly, from the direction of the basketball court, a young boy's voice calls out.

"Hey, Thompson, throw us the ball!" the voice yells out. The boys look toward the basketball court, which is about thirty to forty yards away on a slight hill. Standing on the grass near the edge of the court are three boys, about the same age. The boy in the center, who called out Brad's name, along with the other two, one on each side, impatiently wait with their hands on their hips.

"Sure," Brad responds. He stops spinning the basketball

and tosses it up in the air. Then he catches it with one hand, and with a continues motion, he gives it a strong throw.

Near the court the three other boys watch the ball zip through the air as it heads straight toward them. The basketball rapidly approaches the group as the boy in the center gets wide-eyed in anticipation of catching the flying object. He quickly reacts and catches the ball, but the force is so strong that he stumbles backward and crashes into his two friends. Almost instantly all three crash to the ground like falling bowling pins.

Meanwhile, back at the swing set, JJ and Calvin are laughing hysterically as Brad stares out toward the three boys on the ground.

"Strike!" Brad calls out. The boys share a smile and a laugh. JJ looks toward the parking lot.

"Finally, Amy's here," JJ says.

At the playground parking lot, a newer red Ford Explorer rolls to a slow stop. The driver's side back door flies open as Amy quickly gets out of the vehicle and closes the door. The vehicle backs up and slowly drives away as Amy waves goodbye to her friend.

"Bye! See y'all soon!" Amy yells out as the SUV drives off.

Back at the swing set the boys are looking out toward the parking lot. Calvin gives JJ a curious look.

"What's up?" Calvin asks as Brad perks up to the sight of Amy. JJ calmly gazes out toward the parking lot as he waits for his sister.

"My mom is busy for a couple of hours, so Amy needs to hang out for a while…not too long," JJ replies as Amy walks up to the boys and gives Calvin a smile.

"Hi, Calvin," Amy says. Then she gives Brad a snobbish look. "Hi, weirdo, nice lucky hit."

Brad will take almost any kind of attention from Amy as he sports a smile.

"Thanks! It was nothing," Brad responds as Amy flashes a big grin.

"Oh, it was more than nothing. It was lucky," she says as the group share a chuckle.

Then out of nowhere, the wind starts to pick up, and in the background desert, debris begins to blow across the park. The boys quicky lose their smiles and look concerned as JJ scans the area.

"Hmm…the wind is picking up, and quick!" JJ announces as Calvin nervously checks the surroundings.

"Yeah, I noticed," Calvin mutters out loud. Brad appears deeply worried and starts to get fidgety. He gently smacks his right palm against his forehead.

"No way! Please, no way!" a troubled Brad cries out. Amy rears her head back and looks puzzled at Brad's demeanor.

The wind is quickly getting stronger and begins to howl. The trees and bushes rustle in the ever-growing wind. Within moments, the skies start to darken, and the trees are now intensely swaying back and forth. Tumbleweeds race across the playground like a pack of wild horses as the skies get darker and darker.

Back at the swing set the boys and Amy gather close together. They look frightened and share apprehensive expressions as the weather rabidly deteriorates around them. The blast of wind sends the swing set seats bouncing in all directions. Suddenly, Brad gets wide-eyed as he points to the south.

"Oh no, look!" Brad screams out. "A giant dust storm!"

In the southern horizon, a massive wall of dust is rolling across the desert and bearing down toward the group.

The group remains huddled close together as the wind continues to pick up strength, and the howling becomes almost deafening. JJ, Brad, and Amy's hair are blowing wildly in the wind when suddenly, JJ's cowboy hat starts to blow off his head. He's able to grab his hat, but the Inka bandana sails away.

Calvin whips his backpack around to his front side and pulls out his yellow Eagle Scout neckerchief and hands it to Amy.

"Here, Amy, cover your eyes, nose, and mouth!" an anxious Calvin says. Amy shares a frightened smile with Calvin and grabs the neckerchief. Having spent so much time around horses and dust on the family ranch, Amy quickly places the neckerchief in position. Her hair is blowing wildly, but JJ sees his sister is perplexed as he worries about her safety.

"Amy, stay close!" JJ yells out above the howling wind. Amy cups her hands to protect her eyes and gives JJ a puzzled look.

"JJ, this storm is terrible, and it happened so fast!" a frightened Amy cries out. JJ tries to give his sister an assuring smile, but he knows they're in trouble and he must think fast.

"Come on, guys, we need to find some shelter and now!" JJ commands as he grabs the rope and scans the area. But there's not much, if any, shelter on the playground except the usual playground equipment, which won't be much help. Then Calvin points toward a large pile of rocks located behind the group to their left.

"Hurry, let's get behind that pile of rocks!" Calvin calls out. JJ and Brad nod as the group makes a mad dash toward the rock pile. The dust whips through the air as JJ holds his sister's hand and leads the way. Within a second or two, JJ and Amy dart up to the rock pile, immediately followed by Calvin and Brad.

"Quick, get down!" JJ yells out as the group huddles together. Almost immediately, their position is engulfed by the massive wall of dust as the rock pile vanishes from sight. The howling is tremendous, and the wind is ferocious with no end in sight. But no sooner does it seem as bad as it can get than the wind starts to ease up, revealing the pile of rocks.

CHAPTER THREE

BACK IN TIME

The sound of hundreds of chirping birds and the buzzing of millions of insects fills the air. The surrounding landscape has changed from desert to knee-high grass with boundless small bushes and Joshua trees scattered throughout the area. A small path in front of the rock pile leads to a dense forest with a second path branching off toward the low land near a large pond.

Suddenly, JJ pops his head up from behind the rock pile. He's covered in dust and immediately gets wide-eyed. A second later, Calvin pops his head up, and like JJ, he gets wide-eyed and looks in shock.

"Oh no!" Calvin lets out as he scans the surroundings with JJ.

"Oh yeah!" JJ follows as he shakes his head in disbelief.

Brad and Amy are still crouched down behind the rock but can sense the panic.

"Don't tell me it happened…again!" Brad cries out. "Say it ain't so!" Amy gives Brad a puzzled look.

"Okay, weirdo, what are you talking about?" Amy asks. "What happened again?" Brad puts his hand on the side of his head and gives Amy an empty stare while shaking his head.

Meanwhile, JJ and Calvin can only gaze out where the park used to be with blank faces.

"It happened again," a somber JJ mutters out loud as Brad and Amy slowly raise their heads up from behind the rock pile. Brad cringes, still holding his head. Amy quickly drops her jaw, appearing highly baffled. What she doesn't need is Brad starting to freak out as he begins to walk erratically in small circles.

"No, this can't be…Not again!" an anxious Brad calls out. Amy looks perplexed as she glances at Brad, then she gives JJ a serious look.

"JJ, what's going on? Brad is scaring me, and where are we?" Amy asks as she looks around. JJ and Calvin can only stare out in disbelief at the new surroundings as Amy wedges herself between the boys, gently grabbing JJ's arm. Behind them, Brad continues to pace in a small circle, holding his head in shock.

JJ and Calvin share a confused glance, then stare back out toward the strange environment. Brad, who has finally calmed down enough to join the group, appears mesmerized and bewildered along with the others. A loud screech resonates through the air, along with the multiple insect noises and bird chirping that only seem to be getting louder. Amy sports a near panic expression as she looks up to her brother.

"JJ, what is this place?" Amy asks. "And why is it so chilly?" JJ gives his sister an encouraging smile and hands her his vest.

"Don't worry, Amy. I'll explain later," JJ responds as he looks at Calvin and Brad, then to the forest. "Let's go," he says as he starts to hike up the path, followed by Calvin. Brad leans forward and gives Amy a smile.

"Yeah, Amy, don't worry. I'll save you," Brad states. Amy rears her head back and gives Brad a wry grin.

"Right, Brad, that will be the day…weirdo," Amy sarcastically responds. Then suddenly, she gets bug-eyed as terror covers her face.

"Br—Br—Br—Br—, sn—sn—sn," a horrified Amy stutters out. Brad gives Amy a befuddled look.

"Brrrr, snnn…what?" Brad responds. Amy is speechless and can only repeatedly point her finger in the direction over Brad's left shoulder. Brad looks confused and slowly turns his head and comes face-to-face with the head of a huge black snake. The hissing of the snake pierces the air as its red forked tongue whips around Brad's nose.

Brad is cross-eyed as he stares at the wicked tongue. Then the snake slowly rears its head back and opens its mouth as wide as a volleyball and big enough to swallow all of Brad's head. Brad is petrified as a look of doom covers his face.

"Ahh!" Brad screams as his eyes roll back, starting to faint. With the snake ready to strike, a lasso suddenly whips over its head and quickly tightens around its throat. In a flash the snake is flung into the tall grass and slithers away. JJ and Calvin run up to Brad and Amy, who holds Brad up by the shoulders while he slowly regains consciousness. Brad quietly moans as Amy, JJ, and Calvin stare deadpan out toward their new surroundings.

"Where are we?" a lost Amy asks.

The skies are sunny, but the climate is wetter with cooler temperatures. Because of an average rainfall of approximately forty inches per year, the landscape is abounded by a variety of vegetations. The open areas are covered with tall grass, with scattered cypress, Joshua, and mesquite trees. The mountain ridges are green and lush with plant life. Ahead of the group, there is a forest with an assortment of pine, oak, and hickory trees. Some of the tall trees are noted with long, dangling vines from top to bottom. At the bottom of the basin, a pond is surrounded by a variety of colorful bushes, with reeds and cattails along the banks of the pond. Mesquite trees have populated the area, as the pod seeds serve as a food source for both animals and humans. Animal excrement with pods seeds remains provide nature's way of germinating and growing a new tree.

In the background is a mountain range that will be named South Mountain Park in 1924, and to the west, another range runs north to south. The Spanish will call it the Sierra Estrella, or the Star Mountains. To the south, grassy plains diminish into rolling sand dunes as they fade into the open horizon. The group continues to inexpressively gaze out toward the landscape as flocks of various bird species crisscross throughout the sky. The boys know they're back in time but haven't figured out how far back the storm has taken them as they look for clues. Calvin flashes a concerned expression as he turns to JJ.

"So, what do you think?" Calvin asks. JJ sports a determined look as he scans the area.

"To the high ground, this pond will attract too many critters," JJ replies. Calvin looks puzzled.

"Critter?" an anxious Calvin says. "You mean like scorpions?" JJ shrugs.

"Yeah, Calvin, scorpions that are a foot long!" Brad jokingly informs. "And big snakes." Brad gives JJ an inquisitive look. "In what direction?" a curious Brad asks.

Suddenly, the group hears a loud roar, much like an elephant. JJ squints and looks in deep thought. Calvin, Brad, and Amy are taken by the sound of the roar and look bewildered. Then the roar fills the air again, and the three share an apprehensive glance, but JJ confidently nods.

"Hmm…something tells me we should follow that roar," JJ proclaims. Amy crosses her arms and looks worried.

"I'm scared, JJ. Are you sure?" an uneasy Amy asks as Brad flashes a questionable expression at JJ.

"Yeah, dude, are you sure?" Brad asks when suddenly, a loud, thunderous roar of a large cat, like a tiger or lion, echoes throughout the basin area. Brad gets wide-eyed as he scans the area.

"Okay, let's go!" an anxious Brad replies as Calvin checks his compass.

"Well, the first two roars came from the south," Calvin informs as he points south. The group shares a nod and begins to walk up the small path that leads to the forest. But unbeknownst to the group, they walk past a human foot impression embedded in the trail.

Chapter Four

BIG MAMA

It's later in the day, and the group has been slowly and cautiously walking the trail for about an hour. Some of the trails lead into the forest and some parts along the edge. High above the group, against a bright blue sky with slightly scattered gray clouds, two huge birds that resemble condors circle directly over the boys and Amy. The monster birds have shiny black feathers with wingspans of twenty feet or more. Short white feathers circle the base of their long pink necks, and their heads are also pink with black beady eyes. The beaks and legs of the huge creature are leathery yellow in appearance, with twelve-inch-long deadly black claws.

The monster birds don't go unnoticed by the boys as they look up toward the huge birds. Meanwhile, Amy is lagging behind as she admires some colorful flowers. JJ gives Calvin a curious look.

"So, Calvin, any thoughts?" JJ asks as he turns his head and looks toward Amy. "Hey, Amy, stay close!" JJ yells out. Calvin pushes his glasses off his nose and sports a confident smile.

"Well, the good news is, at least they're not pterosaurs," Calvin calmly states. Brad flashes Calvin a smirky expression.

"Nice. That makes me feel a lot better. Dude, like, what do you mean by good news?" an irritable Brad responds. Calvin nonchalantly glances at Brad.

"We don't want to be back in the Mesozoic Era, you know, the time of the great dinosaurs," Calvin states as the boys stare at the birds.

"Don't matter what era…if we don't get back home," Brad mutters to himself.

"Maybe they're Teratornis," Calvin adds as Brad shakes his head and rolls his eyes.

"Whatever, Calvin. They look like monster birds to me!" an annoyed Brad replies. Calvin sports a big smile.

"Exactly! The word 'Teratorn' comes from the Greek word 'Teratornic,' which means monster bird," Calvin explains. At this point Brad has had it and just shakes his head with a wry expression.

"I feel so much better now," Brad replies as JJ lets out a soft chuckle.

Suddenly, the elephant-like roar is louder and closer, but now it sounds almost desperate. JJ gets wide-eyed, then gives Calvin and Brad a serious look.

"Come on! We're getting closer!" an eager JJ announces. In the background Amy still lags behind as she enjoys the smell of the different flowers. JJ turns around and looks at Amy.

"Hurry up!" a perturbed JJ calls out. Overhead, another bird has joined the two.

So, the group continues their hike through the forest until they come upon an open area surrounded by tall bushes. JJ slowly emerges from behind a large bush. He gives Calvin,

Brad, and Amy a serious look as the three are crouched down behind JJ, watching intently. Suddenly, Brad gets wide-eyed and does a double take.

"Dude, check out the giant armadillo!" an excited Brad says as he taps Calvin on the shoulder. "It's the size of a golf cart!" Calvin and Amy look out toward the large creature that's rumbling through the tall grass about thirty yards away. Calvin pushes his glass off his nose and nods.

"It's a glyptodon, and they went extinct about ten thousand years ago," Calvin informs as he sports a curious expression, pondering his statement. "Very interesting," he adds. Amy's eyes light up as she gazes out toward the horizon.

"Wow, do you see how big those buffaloes are?" a startled

Amy calls out. The size of the roaming herd catches Brad's attention.

"Those are some big buffaloes! They're standing over seven feet tall!" an intrigued Brad adds. Calvin gives the two the "I'm going tell you something" look.

"Actually, they're bison and not buffaloes. The early settlers called them buffaloes, and it's kind of stuck," Calvin informs with a smile. JJ turns around and gives the group a stern look.

"Shhh…Be quiet!" JJ orders as he slowly begins to look around the bush toward the open area. He cautiously creeps around the bush, scanning the surroundings. Then unexpectedly, he widens his eyes and drops his jaw.

To JJ's surprise, a large woolly mammoth stands alone in the open area. The animal's back left foot appears to be wedged between a pile of large rocks as the huge beast is trapped and struggles to free itself. Then the animal raises its head and thrusts its giant tusk toward the sky, letting out a desperate, thunderous roar.

Back at the bushes, JJ is astounded and looks in total awe. Calvin, Brad, and Amy are startled at JJ's behavior and curiously peek around the bush. Within a second, all three widen their eyes and drop their jaws.

"Unbelievable! It's a woolly mammoth!" an astonished JJ proclaims. Calvin leans closer to JJ as Brad and Amy look out at the amazing sight.

"Just what I thought. We're at the end of the last glacier, or the Pleistocene period, and the beginning of the Holocene Era," Calvin announces as Brad gives him a wry look and rolls his eyes while shaking his head.

"You're on a roll today, Calvin. What are you saying?" a perturbed Brads asks. Calvin gives the group a serious look.

"From what I've seen, we're back in time about ten thousand years ago. Give or take, a thousand or two," Calvin states. "Besides, there's no saguaro cacti." Amy walks up to JJ; she looks frightened and puzzled.

"What does he mean we're back in time?" a confused Amy asks. Brad rears his head back and gives Calvin a precarious look.

"Dude, like, what do you mean we're back ten thousand years, and what's up about the saguaro cactus?" an anxious Brad asks as he scans the area. JJ feels he needs to step in; he sees Amy is getting really scared, and Brad is becoming unsettled. JJ gives Brad and Amy a reassuring smile.

"Look, the saguaro cacti weren't around Arizona until about eight thousand years ago in the Tucson area. It's Calvin talk. He was just using it for a time reference," JJ calmly states. Brad gets it and shrugs. But Amy is troubled and confused.

"Why are we here, JJ?" a puzzled Amy asks. JJ gives his sister a gentle smile as he ponders why the Magical Storm has brought them to this time.

"I don't know right now, but I know the storm brought us here for a reason and a purpose. We just need to stick together," JJ adds as Amy grows more on edge.

"A reason!" Amy responds. "A purpose!" Brad gives Amy a slight grin.

"It's not the first time," Brad says, which just adds to Amy's confusion as she gives Brad a questionable look.

"What?" Amy fires off. "Not the first time?" She just shakes her head and looks away. Brad looks up toward the sky and flashes a concerned expression.

"Hmm…closer," Brad mutters to himself.

The three monster birds continue to circle overhead and have descended closer to the group's location.

Meanwhile, in the open area, the mammoth struggles to free its foot. The beast grunts and lets out a roar in desperation as fatigue starts to creep in.

JJ intensely stares out toward the animal. Calvin, Brad, and Amy look overwhelmed with amazement as they watch the animal.

"That woolly isn't going to last long if we don't help," a concerned JJ says. Brad gives JJ a questionable look. He knows JJ's love for animals and knows what he is thinking.

"Dude, I know you want to be a vegetarian someday, but come on," an anxious Brad says. Calvin rolls his eyes and gives Brad a wry look as he shakes his head.

"Man, that's veterinarian, not vegetarian. Geez!" an annoyed Calvin grumbles. JJ continues to stare out toward the animal, then hand signals everyone to sit tight.

"Wait here," JJ says. Amy flashes a worried expression and grabs her brother's arm.

"Be careful," a concerned Amy responds. JJ gives his sister a confident nod and slowly starts to walk from behind the bush. Cautiously, he enters the open area shared with the mammoth. Then he stops walking, and as nonthreatening as he can be, he puts his hands to his side and calmly approaches the huge beast.

The mammoth curiously squints as it apprehensively raises its head. JJ steadily walks directly in front of the mammoth. The beast suspiciously inspects JJ as it lowers its head and stares at JJ with its large eyes.

Back at the bushes, Calvin, Brad, and Amy anxiously watch the interaction between JJ and the mammoth.

"He's nuts," Brad mutters to himself as he shakes his head.

JJ and the mammoth are looking at each other eye-to-eye. There's a slight tension in the air, but JJ can sense the animal knows he is there to help. At that moment JJ gently pats the mammoth's trunk.

"Okay, I think you know I'm harmless. Let me look at that foot," JJ says. He then starts to walk toward the trapped foot, as the mammoth turns its head, its eyes constantly following JJ's every step.

JJ makes his way next to the huge woolly leg of the mammoth and examines the situation. He tries to move the animal's foot, but it doesn't budge.

"Ugh," he grunts out. "No luck. I'll try the rocks," JJ mutters to himself. He reviews the four large rocks that have entrapped the beast's foot. He begins to tug on one of the rocks but can barely move it. He grunts and groans with his efforts when suddenly, he loses his grip and falls on his butt. The large rock falls back into its original position, causing the beast to let out a thunderous roar. Then JJ steps back to the rocks and reexamines the predicament.

"Forget it. I got to get the guys," JJ concludes. So, he walks in front of the large mammoth and gently pats the animal's trunk as he stares directly into the beast's eyes. "I'm going to free you, Big Woolly, but I need my friends," JJ announces. The mammoth curiously squints as JJ glances out toward the bushes that hide Calvin, Brad, and Amy.

Back at the bushes, the group looks in awe as they watch JJ. They see he's looking toward them when his voice calls out.

"Okay, guys, come out nice and easy," JJ's voice rings out. Calvin and Brad share an apprehensive glance, then Brad looks out toward JJ.

"Dr. Dudelittle, are you sure about this?" a reluctant Brad calls out.

JJ almost looks small standing next to the mammoth's huge head, with a shoulder height nearly fifteen feet tall.

"Yeah, just be calm and take your time…and bring some branches from the bushes," JJ replies.

Calvin, Brad, and Amy cautiously creep up toward the mammoth, with Amy holding a nice bundle of bush branches. The group is only about ten feet away when the mammoth lifts its head and lets out a rumbling roar. The sound is threatening, and the group freezes as panic covers their faces. However, the animal lowers its head as JJ begins to gently rub the mammoth's trunk. He signals for the group to come forward.

"Stay calm. Woolly was just saying hello," JJ says. Calvin and Brad share a dubious glance.

"Well, if that was hello, I'd hate to be around for a get lost," Brad mutters to Calvin.

"You're telling me," Calvin responds.

Amy slowly walks up to the mammoth and offers the branches to the animal. The huge beast quickly grabs the branches with its snout and shoves the meal in its mouth. Then the mammoth lets out a mild grunt, as if to say thanks. The group shares a chuckle and feel relieved as they pet the mammoth's trunk. JJ gives Brad a serious look.

"The poor animal's back left foot is trapped in a pile of rocks. It's kind of sketchy looking, but we need to try to pry it loose," JJ announces. Calvin, Brad, and Amy simultaneously lean their heads to the right and look. Together, they curiously examine the mammoth's back left leg.

"Let me try," Brad says. "I'll probably get tromped on." He positions himself next to the large rock and begins to tug on the object with mighty effort, but the rock doesn't budge. Then he pushes on the rock with his legs braced against a large rock for support. But again, among Brad's grunts and groans, the rock still doesn't budge.

"Argh! Nothing!" a frustrated Brad grumbles out. He looks at the group. "What are we going to do?" Brad asks as JJ stares at the rocks.

Meanwhile, Calvin is holding his chin between his thumb and index finger as he contemplates the situation. Then he pushes his glasses off his nose and gives the group a confident smile.

"I got it! Leverage!" Calvin proclaims. JJ, Brad, and Amy all look at Calvin with puzzled expressions as they share a glance with one another.

"Leverage!" the three say together as Calvin smiles and picks up a long stick.

"We'll use the mammoth's own strength to pry the rocks loose. All we need is a long vine and a strong branch," Calvin explains. JJ sports an inquisitive look.

"So, what's your plan?" a curious JJ asks. Calvin nods and takes a quick glance at the animal, then he begins to draw in the dirt.

"Here, this is what it will look like," Calvin responds as he draws his idea in the dirt. After a couple of minutes, Calvin's sketch is completed.

The group huddles together over the drawing as JJ nods and smiles.

"Okay, the vine is tied to Big Woolly's tusk, then it wraps around a tree, and comes back to a branch that's wedged between a couple of rocks causing the problem, right?" JJ asks. Calvin nods as JJ continues to study the drawing.

"So Big Woolly raises its head, creating forward tension on the vine, which causes the branch to move the rocks, hopefully giving Woolly's foot some room to free itself," JJ concludes as Calvin gives JJ the thumbs-up sign.

"That's your part—you need to get Big Woolly to raise its head," Calvin explains. He then looks at Brad, who is still checking out the drawing. Brad senses the silence and rolls his eyes toward Calvin, who gives him a smile.

"And?" Brad says, knowing his part is next.

"I need you to find a big, solid branch and a real long vine from a tree," Calvin announces as Brad flashes a smile with a thumbs-up. Amy gives Calvin a quizzical look.

"What should I do?" Amy asks. Calvin gives Amy a serious look.

"Look, Amy, this is really important. When Brad and I are pushing on the branch, as soon as the rocks separate, you got to jam a nice size stone between them," he says with an urgent voice. Amy perks up, knowing the importance of her task as the plan matches the drawing.

"Oh, I get it, so the rocks don't fall back in place," Amy concludes as the group shares a smile and nods in agreement.

After about an hour or so later, the plan is ready to unfold. Big Woolly has the vine tied to its right tusk, with JJ in position. He has one hand on the tusk, keeping the animal calm, and his other hand is holding some long branches with leaves at the end.

The vine loops around a tall tree about twenty yards away at the perimeter of the forest, then extends to the large branch that is wedged between the two biggest rocks. Calvin and Brad have just finished double-checking the vine knot at the branch and are set to go. Amy is standing close by, holding a rock about the size of a softball and is also ready for action. Calvin and Brad share a nod, and Calvin looks out to JJ.

"Okay, that should do it. Looks like the drawing," Calvin proclaims. JJ, standing in front of the mammoth, is keeping the branches with the leaves low but ready to offer the snack and motivation. JJ flashes a determined look.

"All right, get ready!" JJ says. "It's the carrot-and-stick routine!" At that moment, with Calvin and Brad in position, JJ slowly maneuvers the branches directly in front of the mammoth's mouth as he rattles the offering, teasing the beast to respond.

"Come on, come on," JJ encouragingly calls out as he continues to shake the branches right in front of the animal's eyes, raising the branches and leaves higher and higher. Then the plan starts to work as the mammoth's eyes begin to follow the offerings, and its huge head begins to rise. The vine starts to tighten with the sound of it stretching, and like a chain reaction, it gets tighter as the tusk lifts higher in the air. Calvin and Brad are anxiously watching the vine tighten at the large branch, knowing they will soon be bracing themselves against the branch. They share a nod and get into position. Within seconds the tension on the vine creates vibration, and the two boys give it everything they've got, along with grunts and groans.

"Ugh!" the two grumble out.

"Come on, Brad, just a little more!" Calvin calls out in encouragement. Brad gives Calvin a determined look, then lowers his head and readies for an extra push.

"Argh!" Brad grunts out. Then suddenly, the branch wedged in the rock pile starts to inch forward.

At the other end, JJ is standing on his tiptoes, stretching out as tall as he can to get the leaves as high in the air as possible. He shakes the branches, teasing the animal to get just one more inch of lift.

"Just a little more, Woolly!" JJ coaches. "We can do this!"

Meanwhile, back at the trapped leg, Calvin and Brad are busting gut when finally, the two large rocks have significant separation.

"Now, Amy!" an exhausted Calvin yells out. Amy doesn't waste any time and quickly darts up to the pile of rocks, jamming her rock between the separation. Calvin and Brad let go of the branch and share an urgent look. Without hesitation they start to push on the woolly's leg to help the animal move its leg while the opportunity exists.

The huge mammoth is puzzled at first as it attentively watches the boys push on its leg. Then it realizes what's happening and gets wide-eyed as it lifts its leg from the rock pile. Calvin and Brad keep pushing, and suddenly, the foot breaks free, sending the two boys tumbling to the ground. The mammoth realizes it's free and shakes its head while letting out a tremendous roar.

Unexpectedly, from some bushes at the other end of the open area, a squeaky toot of a roar is heard, completely surprising everyone. The group shares a glance, then curiously stares at the shaking bush. Suddenly, a baby woolly mammoth, about four feet high, comes rushing out of the bushes and runs up to the big mammoth. The baby rubs its body up against the mammoth's big legs, and the huge beast gently strokes the baby with its trunk. The group watches in awe as they witness this prehistoric act of tenderness.

"It's her baby!" an excited Amy calls out. "She's not Big Woolly! She's Big Mama!" The group shares a smile as Calvin suspiciously looks up to the sky.

High in the sky, a fourth monster bird has joined the other

three as they circle over the group.

Brad has joined Calvin as they both observe the four large birds overhead.

"Hmm…that explains the Teratornis," Calvin states.

"Well, if that was the case, I'm glad we freed Big Mama," Brad responds as they stare up in the sky.

Meanwhile, JJ and Amy watch Big Mama and the baby trot toward the forest. Right at the tree line, Big Mama stops and turns her head, looking straight at the group. She raises her huge head and trunk into the air, letting out a thunderous roar. Then the animal turns its head and continues to walk into the forest with the baby at her side. Within a moment Big Mama and her baby slowly fade away into the dense forest. The group watches the two animals disappear, and suddenly, they hear the high-pitched squeak from the baby. They share a smile and a laugh.

Beyond the forest, mountain ranges line the landscape, with the higher plains full of flowing, tall grass. A herd of bison, much like today but larger, roams the plains. To the distance south, the grassy plains become rolling sand dunes, and to the southwest, the Sierra Estrella mountains line the horizon.

Calvin, Brad, and Amy watch JJ stare at the forest tree line as they wait for their next move. In his own solitude,

JJ contemplates his recent experience with the two animals.

"The last mammoths," JJ quietly mutters to himself before addressing the group. "That was amazing!" JJ proclaims. "But we need to get to the high ground." Calvin promptly gets his compass and looks quickly to the south.

"Well, that way is south," Calvin informs as JJ nods.

"Okay then, let's go…and stay close, Amy," JJ says as Amy sports a wry smile and looks at JJ with her hands on her hips.

"Like, where do you think I'm going?" a sarcastic Amy responds. JJ gives his sister a serious look and points south.

Chapter Five

SEARCHING FOR AMY

It's been about an hour or so as the group hikes a trail close to a forest of mesquite, spruce, and tall pine trees. Adjacent to the tree line, there is a dense roll of various plant vegetation, including an array of beautiful colorful bushes. Unexpectedly, the boys wander upon an open grassy area about the size of a basketball court. They share a smile, believing they're making some kind of progress. Meanwhile, Amy is lagging behind as she observes an eye-catching pink flower. JJ turns his head around and gives Amy a serious, perturbed look.

"Amy!" JJ shouts. "Get over here!" Amy looks out toward her brother and can sense he is getting upset with her.

"All right," Amy replies as she sniffs the pink flower one more time. Then she takes off with some quick steps to catch up with the boys, who are about thirty yards ahead.

But up in the sky, things have changed. The boys haven't noticed that the huge condor-like birds have descended and are much closer overhead. Then the pink head of the largest bird appears to be looking downward as a close-up of its dark, beady eye reveals an image of Amy. The monster birds are predators, and predators look for the weak, the strays, and the vulnerable. To the giant birds, Amy looks vulnerable, and within seconds the largest of the birds quickly swoops down toward Amy. The bird's legs are set forward, and its large, eight-inch claws are spread out. The creature lets out an ear shrieking *caw* as it grabs Amy by the vest and lifts her off the ground. The boys are baffled when they hear Amy's desperate scream.

"Help!" Amy yells out as the boys quickly turn their heads, only to see the bird flying away with Amy. The sight of Amy and the bird sends them into shock, their jaws dropping as they watch the large bird slowly gaining altitude with loud whooshes of air with each flap of its giant wings.

"JJ, help, help!" Amy screams out as she wildly kicks her legs and swings her arms. JJ's face is covered in panic, but he quickly shakes it off and makes a desperate dash toward Amy. Calvin and Brad don't hesitate and take off with JJ. The three boys frantically chase after the bird, which continues to gain altitude. Brad passes JJ as he dives in the air, but his outstretched hand just misses Amy's shoe. He crashes hard into the ground and tumbles to a stop. Brad lets out a grunt as JJ jumps over him, reaching helplessly for his sister. But it's too late as the monster bird flies away with Amy, her screams fading as the bird's victory caws echo throughout the forest area. The boys gather, looking totally despondent. JJ is frantic but realizes he must maintain himself or all is lost, including Amy.

"Quick! We got to follow that bird!" JJ yells out as he starts to run down the trail. Calvin and Brad share a dubious glance, then quickly take off, following JJ.

In the southern skies on the horizon, a small speck of a bird carries Amy. Slowly, the bird banks to its right and flies away in a southwest direction.

It's been about a half hour, and high above the ground on a steep cliff, a large bird's nest built out of large sticks and branches rests on a tree trunk protruding about twenty feet from the cliff wall. The nest is about ten feet in diameter with six feet high walls. The location of the nest allows for an unobstructed view of the southern plains for hunting and is in a great defensive position.

Suddenly, the monster bird flies directly over the nest and circles three times before aggressively flapping its wings to perform an aerial stop. A split second later, the bird releases its claws and drops Amy inside the nest and swiftly flies off. Shaken but unharmed, Amy quickly realizes she shares the nest with three large light brown bird eggs.

"Oh no! I got to get out of here!" Amy cries out. She quickly gathers herself and frantically climbs up the wall of the nest and peeks her head over the side. Immediately, she rears her head back in shock, her eyes widening.

The ground is hundreds of yards down from the nest. The trees and vegetation appear small. Above the treetops a flock of birds streak across the sky, appearing like tiny moving dots. If there's one thing that's evident, there's no escape for Amy.

Amy flashes a look of doom and drops to the floor of the nest. She feels hopeless and starts to cry.

"I'm trapped," a despondent Amy mutters out loud. In her fear and frustration, she screams out. "JJ, help me! Help me!" She lowers her head and weeps.

Miles and miles away, a trail leads to an open area that's about twenty-by-twenty yards. The area is quiet except for the chirping of birds and is surrounded by tall trees with a variety of plant life making up the underbrush. Suddenly, the boys burst out of the dense forest into the open area. They abruptly stop running to catch their breath, each one panting heavily.

JJ puts his right hand on his forehead and despondently shakes his head.

"I can't believe this!" JJ calls out. Calvin and Brad share a somber glance, feeling for their friend's grief. Brad gives JJ a comforting pat on the back as Calvin checks his compass, but the two boys know that a bird of this size can cover a vast amount of territory, making the search exceptionally difficult.

"Don't worry, JJ, we'll find Amy," an encouraging Brad says. The boys share looks of determination as JJ nods and appreciates his friend's support.

"We can't stop now, fellas!" JJ states as he looks toward the other end of the open area.

"We're ready when you are, JJ!" Brad proclaims as Calvin holds the compass with one hand and points his index finger with the other.

"Southwest," Calvin informs. "That bird headed straight south and then flew southwest." JJ sports a stern look as he gazes out toward a vast mountain range located southwest from their position.

"That creature was headed somewhere to the Sierra Estrella mountains," JJ announces as the boys look out toward the Sierras, but they're not alone.

Chapter Six

NOT ALONE AND NOT FRIENDLY

Unbeknownst to the boys, about fifteen yards away behind some bushes, a human head with straight black shoulder-length hair slowly emerges into view, secretively observing the boys. The figure wears a buckskin headband and a sleeveless buckskin garment. The arms are muscular, and one of the hands holds some kind of object. Then the figure slowly descends out of view.

JJ and Brad are watching Calvin make some adjustments on his compass as they get ready to resume their search for Amy. Suddenly, there's rustling in the nearby bushes that gets Brad's attention.

"What's that?" a curious Brad questions as JJ and Calvin give him a questionable look.

"What's what?" Calvin asks.

Then out of nowhere, a whooshing sound gets louder and louder until a large stone-tipped spear, like the shape of an arrowhead, slams into the ground right next to the boys' feet. The boys share a startled glance, then look out toward the forest.

"I don't think we're alone," Brad nervously mutters out.

"I guess not," JJ replies as Calvin quickly puts his compass in his back pocket and adjusts his glasses.

"Paleo-Indians," Calvin informs as Brad looks at him puzzlingly.

"Who?" Brad asks as he rears his head back at Calvin's announcement.

"The Paleo-Indians migrated to the North American continent almost twenty thousand… or more, years ago through passages in the northern glaciers. They hunted large animals like mammoths and bison. And here in this part of the country, about ten thousand years ago, they were prevalent, much like the animals we've been seeing," Calvin adds as Brad gives him a half grin.

"Well, that's good to know," Brad sarcastically responds as JJ nods.

"They were known as the Clovis culture by the way they shaped their spear tips," JJ says. "Hopefully, this was just a reminder this is their land and moved on."

The boys share a hopeful smile. But it didn't take long before a dozen Paleo-Indian hunters burst out of the forest, screaming and yelling. They're dressed in full buckskin outfits and are armed with spears and war clubs, much like an Indian Tomahawk. The leader, the largest of the group, leads the attack and shakes his war club over his head. He's also the only one who wears a headband.

The boys stare wide-eyed and drop-jawed at the sight of the charging natives. They share an urgent glance and quickly take off in a mad dash across the open area to the forest, with the Paleo-Indians in hot pursuit. The whooshing sound of spears fills the air as the boys run for their lives. Brad is leading the way, racing down a trail through the forest's underbrush, aggressively swiping away small branches and large leaves out of his way. He turns his head around to look for JJ and Calvin.

"You guys behind me?" an anxious Brad calls out. Directly behind him is JJ, but Calvin is lagging behind a few steps. The boys' faces look desperate as they pant hard with grunts and groans. JJ turns to look for Calvin.

"Keep up, Calvin!" JJ cries out. Calvin sports a look of panic as he takes a quick peek at the Paleo-Indians. Then he fixes his eyes straight ahead and bears down with a strong, steady run. He slowly starts to pull away from the attackers when he flashes a look of pain.

"Ahh!" Calvin screams out as he crashes to the ground with a loud thud, and a seven-foot spear stuck in his backpack. He lifts his head off the ground and looks ahead toward JJ.

"JJ, I'm hit!" he cries out. JJ and Brad share a frightened look and immediately dart back to Calvin. The two boys run up to Calvin, who's still lying on the ground with the spear stuck in his backpack, and quickly kneel next to their friend.

"Calvin, are you okay?" a worried Brad says as he pulls the spear shaft out and tosses it to the ground. JJ reaches into the backpack and feels around.

"I don't think you're bleeding," JJ announces. Then he takes Calvin's Eagle Scout survival handbook out of the backpack with the large stone spearhead stuck in the center. JJ and Brad share a smile and help Calvin get up off the ground. In the background, the screams and yelling from the Paleo-Indians are getting louder by the moment.

"Let's get out of here!" JJ says as he shares an anxious glance with Calvin. Brad is scanning the area until his eyes catch a medium-sized tree branch that is hanging over the trail up ahead.

"You guys get going. I'll catch up," Brad says. JJ and Calvin nod and take off down the trail, ducking underneath the tree branch. Brad looks down the trail in the direction of the attackers, then runs up to the tree branch. He slowly pulls the branch back that's hanging over the trail about ninety degrees and crouches down behind a bush, making sure he is out of view.

Brad's eyes are fixed with determination as he waits for the Paleo-Indians. As the screaming and yelling get louder and the underbrush starts to rumble, four of the Paleo-Indians burst down the trail. Brad's face looks intense as he lets go of the branch at the perfect moment. The branch makes a loud whooshing sound as it whips back into its original position but not before it smacks the hunters to the ground. Brad quickly stands up and flashes a big smile.

"Four down," Brad mutters to himself. Totally unexpectedly, Brad hears loud yelling directly to his right side. His eyes widen in surprise when the leader charges out of the underbrush, attacking with his war club and closing in on Brad within a split second.

"Grrr!" the leader of the Paleo-Indians growls out as he rushes Brad. He doesn't have time to think, but his training takes over as he grabs the leader by the left wrist, which holds the war club, with his left hand and conducts a judo flip over his right hip, sending the attacker sailing through the air and crashing into the underbrush. No sooner has he dispatched the leader than the bushes start to rustle, and two more attackers come screaming out of the dense forest, charging at Brad with spears pointed.

Brad takes a quick look at the ground and sees the spear he pulled out from Calvin's backpack. He grabs it and gets into a martial arts stance, with his left knee forward and bent at about ninety degrees and his right leg back in his stance. He fixes his eyes on the two attackers and starts to twirl the spear from his left side to his right as the two Paleo-Indians close in. Then without hesitation, Brad whips his spear at the first attackers and knocks the spear out of his hands. Almost instantly, while twirling his spear, he conducts the same tactical maneuver against the second foe, who watches as his spear flies out of his hands toward the dense underbrush. The two Paleo-Indians share a dumbfounded look as Brad lowers his right knee to the ground while twirling the spear over his head. In a split second, he swipes the spear right above the ankles of the two attackers, whipping their feet from under them and sending each one crashing to the ground. Brad looks at the two dazzled Paleo-Indians and then takes a quick look down the trail and back at the two hunters.

"See ya!" Brad says as he darts away down the trail. He hustles down the narrow path, bobbing and weaving while slapping small branches out of his way. Finally, he bursts out into an open area that's about twenty-by-thirty yards. On one side of the area is a huge, tall rock formation, which is encircled by the forest and underbrush. Below the rock formation, Brad spots JJ and Calvin waiting for him. Panting hard, he runs up to his two friends.

"Dudes, I think I lost them!" an exhausted Brad proclaims. "And why are they so mad?"

"I think we ruined their dinner plans for the month by freeing Big Mama," JJ informs. The boys share uneasy smiles when suddenly, the bushes start to rustle.

Slowly creeping out of the forest underbrush are the seven Paleo-Indians, lined up side-by-side and spread out to cover any escape route. The boys' hopeful smiles turn to looks of despair as they share a desperate glance. The Paleo-Indian leader advances toward the boys with his war club in hand and is followed by the other six hunters. As they move forward, the boys slowly step backward with their eyes fixed on the locals. JJ turns his head and looks up at the rock formation.

"We're trapped," JJ mutters out loud.

"Maybe I can trade something," Calvin suggests, whipping his backpack around. But his quick action triggers an immediate response from the Paleo-Indians, who raise their war clubs and ready their spears. JJ and Calvin exchange cautious looks as Calvin calmly pushes his backpack back into its original place. Brad has already calculated his odds and gives JJ and Calvin a dubious grin.

"This doesn't look good," a disgruntled Brad states.

Abruptly, a lone Paleo-Indian burst out of the forest and urgently runs up to the leader. He looks frightened, making grunting sounds and frantically pointing toward the forest. The leader's eyebrows raise as he looks toward the direction of the forest. Then the lone Paleo-Indian places his index fingers, which are shaped like hooks, along each side of his mouth while he continues to hysterically grunt and act fidgety. The leader's eyes grow tense as he looks at the forest, and then the boys.

"Argh!" the leader growls out as he kicks the ground in frustration. He gives his hunters a hand gesture, and immediately, they dash away into the opposite end of the forest. The leader follows his men but stops before the forest tree line, giving the boys an angry look before vanishing into the woods.

The boys share a puzzled look as Brad brings his index fingers to his mouth, mimicking the lone Paleo-Indian.

"So, what does this mean?" a curious Brad asks. JJ and Calvin shrug.

"Beats me," Calvin replies. Unexpectedly, the bushes near the forest tree line start to rustle again, and a deep growling noise can be heard. The boys stare out toward the forest and share a concerned glance.

"Well, I guess our friends are back," Brad comments as the rustling and growling noises get louder. But the boys begin to feel it might be something other than the Paleo-Indians and get wide-eyed with looks of uneasy anticipation. They exchange glances and anxiously start walking backward until they bump into the tall rock formation.

"Nobody moves…Just stay calm," JJ announces.

Then one-by-one, four vicious-looking saber-toothed cats emerge from the bushes. They're led by the biggest cat, which measures close to five feet tall from its claws to its shoulders and nearly eight feet in length. It looks muscular, with a mixture of short brownish fur and ten-inch fangs. The other cats look similar except they're about a foot or so smaller in height and length. The three beasts are lined up behind the big cat and spread-out side-by-side in preparation for the oncoming attack. The panting and growling steadily get louder as the big cat lumbers toward Calvin. Its mouth is full of large teeth, and its slanted eyes sport a mean look as it comes face-to-face with Calvin. The warm, turbulent air that comes out of its dark nostrils blasts in Calvin's face with each breath as drool drips from its mouth. Calvin is bug-eyed and petrified in horror as he takes a big gulp.

"Nice, kitty, kitty…Nice kitty, kitty," a terrified Calvin nervously mutters out loud. Brad gives Calvin a wry expression.

"Dude, nice kitty, kitty!" Brad responds in a sarcastic tone.

The big cat rears its head back and appears ready to strike as Calvin's face tenses with his eyes closed. The situation looks doomed when unexpectedly, Brad conducts a high-velocity roundhouse karate kick, slamming his foot against the big cat's jaw. The animal looks startled but quickly turns its attention toward Brad. The boys share terrified, helpless glances.

"Thanks, Brad, but are you sure that was a good idea?" an anxious Calvin asks.

"Instinct," Brad responds as JJ gives him a questionable look.

"We're going to be extinct if we don't figure out something—and quick!" JJ adds as the big saber-toothed cat slowly paces back and forth with its eyes of death focused on Brad. Behind the big cat, the other three creep in for their meal. The big cat lifts its head and lets out a tremendous roar, which is followed by the other three cats. The air is filled with the thunderous echo from the deafening roars as the big cats crouch low for the imminent assault.

Suddenly, the ground starts to tremble, and the top of the trees start to rustle. The boys and the big cats curiously stare out to the commotion in the forest. Within seconds the rumbling and trembling get louder, and the trees start to shake with leaves sailing in the air. The boys can only wonder as the four big cats guardedly step back.

Then like a locomotive, Big Mama bursts out of the forest and crashes through the underbrush. She lets out an earth-shattering roar and charges straight toward the largest cat.

Big Mama knows what needs to be done, and she doesn't hesitate to act. The big cat is bug-eyed and looks perplexed by the sight of the huge mammoth that's charging headstrong. The boys break out in loud cheers and raise their arms in jubilation, knowing they have been saved.

"All right!" The boys scream out as Big Mama lets out a

monstrous roar. She charges up to the lead cat, and in a flash, she wraps her trunk around its body. Then almost effortlessly, she hurls the beast high into the sky toward the forest. The big cat sails through the air with its legs pointing straight up, looking at the ground with a bewildered expression. Abruptly, without hesitation, Big Mama scoops up one of the other cats and tosses it toward the rock wall formation. The cat slams into the wall and falls to the ground unconscious. The two remaining saber-toothed cats look frightened and intimidated as they share a terrified glance. They want no part of the mammoth and quickly run off into the forest.

The boys run toward their hero, cheering, and shouting for joy. JJ runs up in front of Big Mama's huge head, while Calvin and Brad embrace the mammoth's gigantic leg. JJ flashes a big smile as he looks up to his big friend.

"Thanks, Big Mama!" JJ calls out. Her trunk comes down to JJ's level, and to his surprise her spout flips his hat off. JJ lets out a chuckle to her behavior.

"I'd love to play, but we need to find Amy," JJ explains as a high-pitched, gentle roar comes from the bushes. The baby mammoth quickly trots up to its mother and the boys. They share a smile and pet the small creature.

"Well, I guess we're one big happy family!" Brad proclaims.

"Big, all right," Calvin replies. Big Mama starts to walk away, with the baby at her side. Unexpectedly, she stops and turns her head around, looking at the boys. She whips her trunk around as if trying to tell them something. Then she lets out a roar and continues to lumber into the forest. Just before she enters the forest, she turns her head again and gives the boys a quick peek. JJ flashes a serious expression.

"Wow, I think she's trying to tell us something!" an excited JJ states as the boys curiously gaze out toward the mammoth.

"Maybe she knows where Amy is!" Calvin responds.

"Yeah, I think she does!" Brad says as the boys share a hopeful glance.

"I think she does too!" an encouraged JJ proclaims. "Let's go."

So, the boys dart off to catch up with Big Mama and the baby. They finally feel some encouragement in their search for Amy. Not knowing what to expect, they hold on to hope alongside Big Mama.

Chapter Seven

SAVING AMY

It's midafternoon, and the boys have been riding on Big Mama's back for at least a couple of hours. JJ is in front, followed by Calvin, then Brad as they rhythmically sway to the steady strut of the animal. The baby mammoth chases its mother's tail as its legs work to keep up the pace. The landscape features rolling plains with knee-high grass and Joshua trees dotting the terrain. In the foreground is the Sierra Estrella Mountain range with steep cliff and elevations over four thousand feet. As they travel across the rolling plains, Calvin is busy scanning the surroundings with his binoculars. Suddenly, he sits up straighter and appears engaged in the view.

"Hey…I see something!" an excited Calvin announces. His comment immediately gets JJ and Brad's attention. JJ perks up and looks at Calvin with big eyes.

"What?" JJ replies as the two boys intently watch Calvin, who holds the binoculars with both hands, intently focusing.

"Man, it looks like my Eagle Scout scarf. It's waving like a flag above a huge bird's nest!" Calvin states. JJ eagerly waits for more information as Calvin continues to adjust his binoculars. "Yep, that's my scarf, all right," Calvin enthusiastically adds. JJ breaks out in a big smile as he feels encouraged by the good news.

"Amy's letting us know where she at!" an eager JJ says. Brad shakes his head in amazement at what is transpiring.

"She knew, Big Mama knew," Brad mutters out loud as the three share a hopeful smile.

So, the boys, Big Mama, and the baby head toward the huge bird's nest that's about a mile away. They're filled with relief and anxious anticipation to get to their destination, but high above the nest, four monster birds circle in the sky.

It has been close to an hour before the group finally makes it to an open area at the base of a towering cliff far below the nest. The open area is half surrounded by tall trees with long, dangling vines. Big Mama stops and lowers her head, then one-by-one, the boys slide down her trunk to the ground. They walk toward the center of the open area with eyes fixed on the distant nest. Abruptly, Brad trips and tumbles to the ground. He gets up and looks behind him to see a tree root that has come out of the ground and looped back into the surface, forming a horseshoe pattern.

"Who put that there?" an irritated Brad mumbles to himself. He quickly jogs up to JJ and Calvin, who are staring up at the huge nest. Brad joins his two friends, and they all gaze upward.

"Dudes, that's really up there!" Brad says as the boys scope out the nest, which is about two hundred yards up a steep rocky cliff. The nest is positioned on a large branch that is straight out the side of the cliff and is close to twenty feet in length. But ever present are the four monster birds.

The boys continue to stare up at the nest. JJ flashes a determined expression and gives Calvin and Brad a serious look.

"Look, Amy needs to know we're here. So together, on three, we'll shout out her name. Ready. One, two, three!" JJ counts out.

"Amy!" the boys call out together.

Inside the bird's nest, a dejected Amy blankly stares at the three brown eggs that have slowly been cracking, with hatching expected at any moment. Suddenly, she hears her name and perks up, getting wide-eyed. She quickly scales the side of the nest and pops her head over the wall of the structure.

As she peeks over the side, she grabs the stick with the yellow neckerchief and frantically starts to wave it.

"Hurry up! I think I'm going to be lunch any second!" an anxious Amy yells out.

On the ground, Big Mama has joined the boys as all of them stare up toward the nest, leaving the baby mammoth hungry from the long journey to feed on some tall grass. JJ cuffs his hands around his mouth and takes a deep breath.

"Don't worry, Amy, we'll get you!" JJ shouts out with a hopeful voice. Calvin and Brad give JJ a puzzled look, then stare up at the steep cliff wall.

"How?" a curious Calvin asks as Brad continuously stares up toward the nest and then looks at JJ.

"Dude, what do you have in mind?" a bewildered Brad asks. JJ rubs his chin and appears deep in thought.

"Well, I guess I'll have to climb this cliff," JJ mutters out loud. Calvin pushes his glasses off his nose.

"Man, I don't think we have that much time," Calvin responds as he points up toward the four monster birds.

Against a backdrop of scattered white clouds and a bright blue sky, the four monster birds circle above the nest but steadily descend closer to their aerie, or the nest of a bird of prey and Amy.

JJ and Brad share dubious glances as Calvin's eyebrows lower, and his face looks tense. The two boys know Calvin is thinking of something, but they don't know what he has in mind. They watch Calvin as he looks up at the nest and back to the surrounding area. With his focus on the tall tree with the long, dangling vines, he begins to walk backward, still observing the landscape.

"Hey, watch out for the...," Brad says, but before he can finish, Calvin trips over the looped tree root. "Horseshoe loop in the ground!" he mutters as Calvin gets up and looks at Brad.

"What?" he asks Brad as he closely looks at the odd shape of the tree root in the ground.

"Never mind," Brad says as he shares a smile with JJ. Calvin is still looking at the looped root, then nods with a confident grin.

"I got it! Here, we will build the ramp right here!" Calvin announces as JJ and Brad share a confused look.

"Ramp?" they question together.

"A ramp for what?" a curious JJ asks.

"Yeah, for what? And besides, the looped root is in the middle of the area. Isn't it in the way?" a puzzled Brad asks.

"No, actually, it's what we need to hold the vines close to the ground," Calvin mentions. At this point JJ and Brad are still trying to figure out what Calvin has on his mind as they watch Calvin step off distances and gather information.

"Okay, I give…how about some details," Brad states.

"Yeah, Calvin, what's up?" an anxious JJ asks. Calvin flashes a determined expression at JJ and Brad.

"We're going to build a giant bow and arrow!" Calvin enthusiastically announces. Brad sports a dumbfounded look.

"A what?" Brad asks. "A giant bow and arrow, are we going hunting or something?"

Calvin is angling his arm and hand at different degrees as he studiously makes his calculations. He looks at JJ and Brad.

"The bow will be connected to a ramp, which is at about sixty-degree launch angle," Calvin explains as JJ nods, while Brad still looks confused.

"You mean like a crossbow?" a curious JJ asks. Calvin flashes a big smile.

"Exactly! The bow will be strong enough to launch an arrow that's carrying you or Brad, and a long string of vines to the nest and Big Mama will supply the power," a proud Calvin adds. Brad sports a suspicious expression while he stares up at the nest, then he looks at Calvin.

"So…Amy jumps a ride on the arrow?" a quizzical Brad asks.

"Hey, I get it. We get Amy to climb down the long vine," JJ says as Calvin smiles and points his index finger at the nest.

"Better yet, we use a belt and slide down. Like a zip line. It will be faster," Calvin proclaims as he looks up toward the birds. "Besides, look!" The boys glance up at the birds.

The four monster birds continue to fly in a steady circular pattern, but now they're only twenty or thirty yards above the nest and Amy.

The boys share a desperate glance as JJ's face tenses up.

"Geez, I don't think we have much time," a disturbed JJ states. Brad sees his buddy is stressing and feels his anxiety.

"Dude, we'll get Amy," Brad proclaims as he tries to reassure JJ. Calvin gives the boys a serious look.

"Look, we got to act fast!" Calvin states as he picks a long stick off the ground. "Here's the design." Calvin starts to draw in the dirt as JJ and Brad intently watch. After a couple of minutes or so, Calvin is done and lifts the stick from the ground and flashes a big smile. "There, this is what it will look like," Calvin announces as JJ and Brad share an enthusiastic smile.

The drawing reveals a crossbow configuration positioned on a ramp with a fairly steep incline. Located at the top of the ramp is a cylinder-shaped projectile that appears larger toward the front, with a small dot noted in the center-front of the sketch. Small wings are noted at the midsections, with smaller wings at the tail. A vine functions as the bowstring and attached to the bowstring is another vine that runs down the ramp to the ground. The vine then runs through the looped tree root, and after what looks like several feet of slack, the vine is tied to Big Mama's tusk. At the stern or the end of the cylinder-shaped projectile, a vine is connected that leads to a neat circular pile of additional vines.

The boys huddle together, admiring Calvin's design and sharing confident nods.

"Cool and is the little dot on the arrowcraft…me?" a curious Brad asks. JJ gives Brad a grin with a slight smirk.

"You?" JJ quickly responds. Brad gives JJ a pathetic look.

"Come on, dude, I want to save Amy!" Brad states. The three boys share a glance.

"I get it, Brad, but she's my sister," JJ explains. Calvin senses the need to interject and puts his hands up.

"Wait, JJ, you need to stay here with me," an anxious Calvin announces. JJ gives Calvin a wry eye.

"Why?" JJ firmly asks. Calvin gives JJ a serious look as he nods.

"JJ, Big Mama is the key. She has the power to draw the bowstring back. If something goes wrong with that function, we'll fail. You need to be here with her. She'll listen to you. She trusts you," Calvin somberly explains.

JJ stares off to the ground and then looks at Big Mama, who has been watching the boys all along. JJ nods with a tight-lipped grin.

"Okay, I get it," JJ responds. Brad wants to assure his friend and puts his hand on JJ's shoulder.

"JJ, I won't let you down. I'll get Amy back," Brad says with a confident smile. JJ returns the smile and gives Brad and Calvin a fist bump.

"Okay then, let's build this thing!" an eager JJ announces. Calvin looks toward the forest, then whips his backpack around. He reaches in, pulling out a small hatchet with a retractable handle and his Swiss Army knife. He hands the knife to Brad with the saw blade open.

"Brad, cut down a bunch of vines," Calvin says as Brad

grabs the knife.

"JJ, you and I need to gather the branches," Calvin informs, then he brings his thumb and index fingers to his chin, turning his head in a curious fashion.

"Arrow…craft…I like it, arrowcraft. It's got a ring to it," Calvin mutters to himself as the boys scamper off to the forest to gather the supplies, they'll need to build Calvin's vision with the hope of saving Amy.

It's been at least two solid hours, and the large crossbow configuration is positioned at approximately a sixty-degree angle, ready for launch. The ramp has been constructed out of long, straight twelve-foot branches and supported by several X-pattern trestles. The trestles are also made from branches and tied together with smaller vines. In front of the ramp, two twenty-foot branches are strapped together in the center of the frame, serving as the bow.

Resting at the top of the ramp is the arrowcraft, constructed from several long, thin six-foot branches that form the rounded body. The branches are tapered at the ends and held together with duct tape. The bulge in the front-center has a large opening that will function as the cockpit, with smaller X trestles in front and back of the cockpit to support the frame. Stiff leaves are duct taped to twelve-inch branches to form a triangle-shaped pattern that makes up the front wings, with additional leaves at the tail section to act like the feathers on an arrow.

And just like the drawing, a vine is tied to another vine that will pull back and act like a bowstring. The vine tied to the bowstring runs to the base of the ramp, then under the looped tree root, and continues for about thirty feet, where it's tied to Big Mama's tusk. Next to the base of the ramp is a neatly coiled pile of vines that are duct taped together end-to-end and tied to the back of the arrowcraft.

The boys admire their project, but when JJ looks up toward the sky, he sees that the four monster birds have steadily descended closer and closer to the nest where Amy is. He gives Calvin and Brad a desperate look.

"Let's hurry up. Those birds have gotten closer, and I'm sure Amy is really sacred," a concerned JJ says.

The boys share a nod and get ready to launch. Brad quickly climbs up the ramp and into the cockpit. He gets slightly hunched over, ready for takeoff. As Calvin makes some last-minute inspections on the ramp, JJ slowly guides Big Mama into position, preparing her to walk backward to pull on the vines. With everything set to go, Big Mama begins her walk, causing the vines to tighten and steadily lose slack. Soon, the vines start to pull through the looped tree root and begin to draw back the bowstring. Gradually, the arrowcraft starts to slide down the ramp as the sound of the stretching vines fill the air, creating more anxiety for the boys.

Finally, and with much relief, the bowstring and arrowcraft are in maximum position for prelaunch at the base of the ramp. JJ looks over to Calvin, who is cautiously monitoring the situation.

"Calvin, use your pocketknife to cut the vine. That's how we'll initiate the launch," JJ suggests. Calvin nods in agreement and reaches into his pocket for his knife.

"Good idea!" Calvin eagerly responds as he looks up to Brad in the cockpit. "Hey, Brad, you'll need to lean right or left to steer this thing," Calvin explains as Brad flashes a smile and gives Calvin the thumbs-up.

"Let's get Amy!" an enthusiastic Brad replies as Calvin returns the thumbs-up.

JJ is keeping Big Mama calm as Calvin starts to cut through the vine at the base of the ramp.

"Hold it steady, Big Mama," JJ tells the animal. With the bowstring as taunt as possible, Calvin is kneeling at the base of the ramp and methodically cutting through the vine. He looks up at Brad, who is hunched over and ready to go.

"Get ready, Brad. I'm almost through the vine. Five, four, three," Calvin calls out as he keeps working. Simultaneously, in the cockpit, Brad waits for the launch. Suddenly, he sits straight up and flashes a questionable expression as he turns around to look at Calvin.

"Dude, by the way, when I get to the nest how do I—" Brad anxiously tries to ask as Calvin continues cutting away.

"Three, two, one…launch!" Calvin yells out, not hearing Brad. A split second later, the arrowcraft takes off like a bullet, creating a loud *whoosh* as it rips off the ramp.

"Stop this thing!" Brad yells out, finishing his question as his voice quickly fades away. JJ, Calvin, Big Mama, and the baby curiously watch the arrowcraft sail through the air toward the nest.

"So, Calvin, what was Brad trying to ask you?" a curious JJ asks while staring at the arrowcraft.

"Ah…something to do with stopping this thing," Calvin replies as he nods.

"Sounds like a good question," JJ responds as he gives Calvin a curious look. "So how does he stop that thing?" Calvin pushes his glasses off his nose as he squints, flashing a serious look.

"Hmm…I guess I didn't think of that," Calvin concludes as the two boys share a dubious glance.

Meanwhile, Brad is hunched over in the cockpit, the wind whipping his hair and his baseball jersey flopping in all directions as he holds on to his Cubs hat.

"Whoa! This thing is moving!" Brad proclaims as he spots a jagged rock formation directly to the right of his flight path. "Better lean to the left," Brad mutters to himself as he quickly makes the move and then returns to the center position. He looks straight ahead and flashes a confident smile after he sees the yellow neckerchief flapping in the breeze. "Right on target!" an excited Brad says as he guides the arrowcraft between the nest and the cliff.

Then within a second, Brad and the arrowcraft blast through the tight space directly over the extended tree trunk. Twigs and leaves kick up from the turbulent air as the long string of vines follows from the back end of the arrowcraft. Gradually, the arrowcraft starts to lose momentum and creates a descending arch flight pattern. Gravity takes over as the arrowcraft starts to fall from the sky, but with the vines drooping over the tree trunk at a high speed, the arrowcraft begins a series of loops around the tree trunk. The monster birds are startled as the arrowcraft whips around at a blurring speed, getting closer and closer to the nest with each revolution. Then suddenly, the arrowcraft comes to a stop, slowly rocking back and forth while pointing straight downward.

Inside the cockpit Brad's head wobbles, and his eyes are crossed. He blinks and shakes his head to regain his senses as he looks straight down.

"So that's how you stop this thing!" Brad announces, but he is focused on what he came for and looks up toward the nest.

"Hey, Amy, are you okay?" Brad yells out. He realizes he must act fast and quickly climbs out of the arrowcraft's cockpit. Then he carefully walks a few steps on the tree trunk before he begins to scale the side of the nest wall.

He is anxious and worried about Amy, but no sooner has he reached the top of the nest, Amy pops her head up just above the rim, making direct eye contact with Bard. She gets wide-eyed and flashes a big smile.

"Brad! Boy…I never thought I'd be glad to see you!" Amy proclaims as Brad gives her a half grin and nods.

"You'll thank me someday, but right now, we got to get out of here and fast!" an excited Brad states as he points to the sky, where the four monster birds are directly overhead, staring down at the nest.

The four monster birds are circling above the nest with angry eyes. Suddenly, one of the birds makes a sharp, rapid descent and is quickly followed by the other three birds like a pack of dive bombers.

Back at the nest, Amy is desperately trying to climb the steep wall of the nest as she grunts and groans but can't seem to get any footing. Brad is edgy as he watches the birds make their attack, but he quickly realizes Amy needs help.

"Let me help, Amy!" Brad says as he reaches over the nest, and with both hands, he picks up Amy under her armpits, lifting her out of the nest. He quickly places her on the tree trunk as the two share a nervous smile.

"Now what?" a frightened Amy asks.

"Come on, just get ready!" an anxious Brad replies.

Down at the ramp, JJ and Calvin are wide-eyed and drop-jawed as they look up toward the nest. Directly behind them, Big Mama and the baby curiously watch the action. The two boys share a smile.

"It worked!" an ecstatic Calvin calls out.

"That was awesome!" JJ replies as he looks at the remaining pile of vines, then looks at Big Mama.

"I'll need to tie the vines around Big Mama's body. She'll be able to keep the vine tight," JJ says.

"Great idea, and her woolly side will act like a cushion," Calvin adds as JJ grabs the coiled vines and quickly tosses them over Big Mama's back. It doesn't take long for JJ to secure the vines and start to guide Big Mama to walk sideways. Soon, the slack in the string of vines begins to tighten and within seconds becomes taunt. Calvin gives JJ a nod with a thumbs-up, letting him know everything looks good with Big Mama in position. Then he aggressively starts to wave both arms toward Brad and Amy, getting their attention.

"Okay, the vines are tight!" Calvin yells out.

Up at the nest, Brad and Amy have been anxiously waiting for Calvin's signal, while Brad has been busy getting the belt ready.

"Looks like we're getting the go signal from Calvin," Amy informs. Brad has buckled the belt together and flings it over the vine. Then he places his hands through the belt loop to his wrist and holds the belt strap tight.

Suddenly, four black flashes as the birds streak past the nest. The loud whooshes startled Brad and Amy as small twigs and leaves kick up from the turbulent blast of air. The two share a nervous expression as they notice the yellow neckerchief is gone. But Brad quickly gets back to work. With the belt drooped over the vines and his hands secured through the belt loop, he leans forward, giving Amy a serious look.

"Okay, Amy, climb on my back, and hold on as tight as you can!" Brad eagerly instructs. Amy quickly responds, and within seconds the two commence to slide down the long string of vines. They rapidly pick up speed, their heartbeats pounding nervously as they make their escape. Directly behind them, with huge claws spread wide open, the four monster birds swoop down one after another. Each bird relentlessly snaps at Amy with every passing. Brad and Amy are terrified as they slide down the vines like a zip line at high speed. The friction from the vines and the belt is so intense that it leaves a trail of smoke.

Amy feels the presence of a bird so close that she hears

the snapping of its beak right next to her ear. However, as scared as she is, she knows that total panic is not an option.

"Oh no!" screams a frightened Amy. Brad keeps a determined look as takes a quick peek at the smoking belt. His face tenses, knowing that if the belt snaps, it will be the end of them both. He focuses straight ahead and sees the vine line running directly into the side of Big Mama.

"Hold on, Amy! We're almost there!" Brad calls out, trying to encourage Amy. But the birds are angry and relentlessly snap at her flowing hair. She dodges and weaves her head back and forth to avoid any bites. Suddenly, Amy flashes a defiant look as her face tenses up.

"Enough of you, bird!" Amy yells out as she gives the annoying raptor a hard elbow right between the eyes. The bird gets startles and promptly flies away. With the side of Big Mama rapidly approaching, Brad makes a quick head turn to Amy.

"Put your chin on my shoulder and get ready!" Brad firmly commands.

Meanwhile, on the ground, JJ is keeping Big Mama steady as Calvin and the baby gather about ten yards away for the point of contact. All four anxiously and curiously stare up at Brad and Amy, who are speedily getting closer. A second later Brad and Amy streak past Calvin and the baby as they slam directly into Big Mama's thick, woolly fur body. The two bounces off her side and fall to the ground. A moment later they are sitting up, shaken and dazed but unharmed. JJ and Calvin can't believe their eyes as they run up to them with astonished expressions. Calvin runs up to Brad, while JJ tends to Amy.

"Amy are you okay?" an exasperated JJ asks his sister as she shakes her head and gives her brother a blank stare.

"Yeah, I think so," a stunned Amy replies as JJ looks on. Calvin and Brad clasp each other's hands, and Calvin helps his friend off the ground.

"Man, that was superhero!" an excited Calvin says. Brad brushes himself off and straightens his Cubs hat while pulling out a woolly hair from his mouth.

Soon, the group gathers, relieved and feeling fortunate for the outcome. They share smiles and high fives, each knowing an unfamiliar trek lies ahead. Then, in the background, the wind starts to pick up, and they notice that the treetops begin to gently sway in the breeze. JJ flashes an inquisitive expression.

"I think we need to get to the open high ground as soon as possible," JJ says, prompting the group to share cautious but hopeful glances. There's a feeling of slight apprehension among the four, when unexpectedly, the yellow neckerchief floats from the sky and lands on the top of the baby's head. Its eyes look upward, and it lets out a tiny roar. The group shares a much-needed laugh as Big Mama whips her trunk in the air.

Chapter Eight

GOING HOME

A couple of hours later, the boys walk together alongside Big Mama. Calvin has his binoculars around his neck as he checks out his compass. Amy is wearing the yellow neckerchief as a bandana as she walks next to the baby.

The landscape has slightly changed, there are fewer scattered trees, and the prairie grass is shorter. In the background are the mountain ranges where the group left just hours earlier, and in the foreground the prairie grass seems to blend into rolling sand dunes.

Suddenly, the wind starts to blow stronger with a faint howl in the air. Loose grass and dust begin to blow across the open plains. JJ and Brad share a puzzled glance as Calvin brings the binoculars to his eyes. He quickly points to the south.

"Hey, look!" an excited Calvin says as JJ and Brad anxiously follow his command.

In the far distant southern direction, a dark wall of dust lines the horizon and is rolling across the landscape, heading toward the group's location.

JJ and Brad continue to stare out toward the south as Calvin adjusts his binoculars, then pulls them away, giving JJ a confident smile.

"Man, the storm's coming this way!" Calvin announces. JJ gets wide-eyed in anticipation and hope.

"Let's go!" JJ enthusiastically says. "This might be our only chance!" So, the group makes a desperate dash along with Big Mama and the baby. The three boys are running side-by-side when Brad looks at JJ.

"Dude, this is crazy. Usually, we are running from these storms. Now we're running to one," Brad proclaims. JJ nods in agreement.

"Yeah, but we got to give it a shot. Let's hurry!" JJ replies as he turns his head around to find Amy. Amy's a good runner and is closely behind the boys with Big Mama and the baby holding on to its mother's tail directly behind her.

Dust, sand, and debris are blowing intensely across the landscape as the wind gets stronger and the howling louder.

In the southern horizon, the dark wall of dust is closer and much larger. The sky above the storm is hazy as the sunlight fades away.

The group stops running and huddles together while catching their breath. Amy is wearing Calvin's yellow handkerchief to cover her nose and mouth for protection. There are no trees or any large boulder in sight as the dangerous wind steadily blows stronger. JJ and Calvin desperately scan the surroundings, then he flashes a serious expression to Calvin.

"I don't see any shelter!" an anxious JJ announces. Clavin squints and partially covers his mouth with his hand.

"JJ, lets huddle up next to Big Mama's leg!" Calvin suggests.

As the sky darkens with the wall of the storm less than fifty yards away, the group quickly huddles around Big Mama's front left leg. The frightened baby is behind them and rubbing up against its mother's left back leg. Within a second a giant dark wall of dust, like a huge tidal wave, starts to engulf Big Mama and the group. Suddenly, the baby mammoth panics and runs off. With the storm so violent and no visibility, the group and Big Mama are unaware the baby has fled.

After what seems like forever but only a couple of minutes, the storm starts to ease up, and through the dusty haze, the group becomes visible. In the background the South Mountain and the communication towers are in view as JJ scans the familiar surroundings.

"Look! The towers!" a happy JJ announces. Calvin, Brad, and Amy sport a smile as they see the houses, streets, and light poles that make up a nearby neighborhood. The group is gathered in the desert, but they know they're close to home and feel much relieved.

"Dudes, we made it home with no worries," Brad proclaims as Calvin flashed a big smile but then sports a quizzical expression.

"Man, what a strange journey, and why?" Calvin wonders out loud. JJ just shrugs and is happy to be home.

"Well, I guess there's a reason for everything, I suppose," JJ nonchalantly states. Then unexpectedly, the boys hear a familiar grunt and immediately share a bewildered glance. Amy quickly turns around and suddenly looks in shock.

"Big Mama!" a startled Amy shouts out. The three boys promptly turn around, their jaws dropping in surprise.

"What is she doing here?" a puzzled Calvin responds. Brad cannot believe his eyes.

"Dudes!" Brad yells out as JJ can only shake his head.

"Wow! Big Mama, what's going on?" a confused JJ replies.

Amy walks closer to JJ and gives him a worried look.

"JJ, what are we going to do?" a concerned Amy asks as JJ flashes a serious expression.

"We need to hide her, but how?" an anxious JJ suggests. Brad gives Calvin a silly grin.

"Hey, Calvin, maybe you can hide her in your garage. You always wanted a pet," Brad says with a chuckle. Calvin flashes a smirk grin at Brad.

"Oh, and I can take her for evening walks…Please!" an annoyed Calvin replies.

"Fellas, we don't have time for jokes. We need to think of something!" JJ states as Calvin and Brad nod in agreement.

So, the group hastily spend the next several minutes scampering about moving Big Mama from one group of bushes to the next or tossing mesquite branches against her woolly side. The three boys and Amy share doubtful faces as they realize how difficult it is to hide the giant beast.

"Dudes, we're not getting anywhere," an anxious Brad informs the group as they share hopeless grins. Then in the distant background, faint sounds of sirens can be heard, which quickly get louder and louder.

"I don't think we have to worry about it," JJ says as

multiple police cars and emergency vehicles with flashing lights race toward the group's location. The boys gather next to Big Mama as Amy anxiously scans the area. She has a look of desperation as she can't locate the baby, and in the midst of all the commotion, no one noticed the little creature was missing.

"Oh no!" Amy cries out. "Where's the baby?" She covers her face with her hands and starts to cry. "The poor baby!" a despondent Amy says. The boys look puzzled as they search the area.

Then suddenly, an animal control vehicle with flashing lights comes to a screeching stop in front of the group. Immediately, and before the boys could do or say anything, an individual from the vehicle fires a tranquilizer gun at Big Mama. The group is stunned and watches helplessly as a large flatbed truck pulls up and, within a short time, hauls Big Mama away. Within a few seconds, another police vehicle pulls up close to the group. An officer soon gets out. The boys share a glance. Then Calvin and Brad give JJ the "Now what?" look. JJ nods, and with a tight grin, he steps forward to greet the officer.

Chapter Nine

THE WINDS OF EXTINCTION

Dr. Charles, a zoologist in his early sixties and the zoo director, is sitting at his desk holding his bald head with sides that are trimmed with short gray hair. He wears a white shirt with a black tie under his white lab coat. Dr. Charles is totally despondent as he shakes his head while he looks at the headline of a newspaper on his desk that reads: "Rare Blood Disorder Threatens Elephants with Total Extinction." He takes his black wire-rimmed glasses off and blankly stares out toward the window.

"This is so terrible, and there's nothing I can do to save these poor creatures. This disease will wipe out the entire population," a dejected Dr. Charles says. He puts his glasses back on, and with his eyes closed and tight lips, he slams the desk with his fist.

"If this develops to an animal-to-human transmission, it could be a global catastrophe!" A helpless Dr. Charles cries out as he folds his arms and lays his head down. Suddenly, there's aggressive knocking on the door, prompting him to raise his head and look toward his office entrance.

"Yes, come in," a somber Dr. Charles says.

Within a second the door flies open, smacking against the wall. Dashing through the doorway in a frenzy is Dr. Freeman, also a zoologist. He's in his late thirties and is Dr. Charles's assistant. Donning a white lab coat over his white shirt with a black tie and black glasses, he charges up to Dr. Charles's desk. His black hair is messy, and he is very energetic.

"Dr. Charles, I have some truly unbelievable news!" an excited Dr. Freeman says with fidgety fingers and busy hands. "A large woolly mammoth has been found!" Dr. Charles looks up to Dr. Freeman and appears very unimpressed.

"Oh…some bones?" Dr. Charles responds. Dr. Freeman steps closer to Dr. Charles's desk, sporting a big smile.

"No, sir, I mean a real live living woolly mammoth!" a jubilant Dr. Freeman announces. The news quickly catches Dr. Charles's attention, causing him to quickly sit up in his chair with a curious expression.

"What are you saying, Dr. Freeman?" a puzzled Dr. Charles responds.

"I just received a phone call from the police department, and they are bringing the live animal here as we speak!" Dr.

Freeman informs. "Of course, the animal has been tran-quilized." Dr. Charles quickly stands up. He gets wide-eyed and looks totally amazed.

Back in the desert, Calvin, Brad, and Amy watch JJ, who is talking to a policewoman. JJ shakes the officer's hand, and a moment later she gets into her police vehicle. JJ stands and watches the vehicle pull away, then he walks back to the group. Calvin and Brad give JJ a curious look.

"What's up?" Brad asks.

"Well, I told her we were hiking and just came across this hairy elephant, thought it escaped from the zoo," JJ explained as Brad nodded.

"Good move!" Brad responds. Calvin and Brad share a smile and a nod, then Calvin gives JJ a serious look.

"What did the officer say?" a curious Calvin asks.

"They're taking the animal to the zoo for observation," JJ responds. Calvin throws his arms up and flashes a grin.

"No kidding, once they realize they got a ten-thousand-year-old woolly mammoth…they'll be doing a lot of obser-vation!" Calvin proclaims. Amy somberly looks up to JJ.

"But what about the baby?" a concerned Amy asks. The boys all share a serious look as Amy puts her hands to her face and starts to cry.

"I know, the baby won't survive long without her mother," JJ announces as Calvin pushes his glasses off his nose.

"Man, we got to figure out a way to get Big Mama back to her baby!" Calvin responds as JJ rubs his chin in deep thought.

"Look, let's meet at the park first thing tomorrow and come up with a plan," JJ announces. The boys nod in agreement as Amy tugs on JJ's arm.

"What about Mom and Dad?" a concerned Amy asks. JJ gives Amy a serious look.

"Amy, you can't say anything now! Maybe later, but not now, okay?" JJ states. Amy gives JJ a hesitant grin.

"Okay, but just because of the baby," Amy replies. JJ gives his sister a comforting smile.

"It's about the baby, Amy, but we just need to keep quiet for a while," JJ responds.

"Well, I'm just going to play stupid and act like I don't know anything," Brad says. Calvin can't help himself; he turns his head away, putting a hand over his mouth.

"That should be easy," Calvin mutters. Brad gives Calvin a quick glance with squinted eyes.

"What?" Brad questions. Calvin does his best to act innocent and shrugs.

"Nothing…The park, early am," Calvin says. JJ stares off and sports an inquisitive expression.

"Why would the storm bring Big Mama back home with us? It just doesn't make sense," JJ wonders out loud as the group glances bewildered expressions.

It's nighttime at the zoo, and only the nocturnal animals and birds make occasional noise. Under the floodlights in each corner of a fifteen-by-fifteen-yard steel chain-link fence cage, Dr. Charles and Dr. Freeman admire the tranquilized mammoth as it lies on the ground.

"Dr. Freeman, this is absolutely astonishing!" a joyful Dr. Charles says.

"It is, sir," Dr. Freeman responds. Dr. Charles gives Dr. Freeman a serious look.

"Dr. Freeman, you should collect all your lab samples while the animal is asleep. Once word of this gets out… well, this place will be a zoo!" Dr. Charles proclaims as the two doctors share a laugh.

"That was a good one, sir," Dr. Freeman says with a chuckle.

"Well, I'm calling it a night. Check the locks and bolts before you leave, Dr. Freeman."

Chapter Ten

DISGUISE, SURPRISE, AND ESCAPE

It's midmorning as JJ sits on a swing at the park. He sports a confident smile as he gazes out toward the basin area of the park.

Quietly, Calvin and Brad walk up toward JJ, their footsteps catching his attention as he quickly jumps off the swing to meet his friends. He enthusiastically fist-bumps his buddies.

"So how did it go? Anybody's parents say anything about the news of the mammoth?" a curious JJ asks.

"Yeah, my dad said something, but I acted like I didn't hear him," Calvin responds. Brad shrugs.

"Nothing here. How is Amy?" Brad asks.

"Oh, she's just worried about the baby," JJ replies. Calvin and Brad curiously step closer to JJ. The two know JJ and can sense he's on to something.

"So did you come up with a plan?" Calvin asks, excepting a positive response.

"Yep, it's called disguise, surprise, and escape!" a motivated JJ announces. Calvin and Brad get wide-eyed and rear their heads back by JJ's positive statement.

"Okay, let's hear it!" Calvin says with great anticipation as JJ gives the two a smile.

"We're going to get some shag rugs and spray-paint them black. Then we're going to make a baby mammoth costume!" an excited JJ announces. Brad gets drop-jawed and looks dumbfounded.

"What?" Brad responds. Calvin gives JJ a nod and a grin.

"Hmm…the disguise," Calvin says.

"That's right. Look, we got to get inside the zoo to free Big Mama, right?" JJ asks. Calvin and Brad intently listen to JJ and nod in agreement. "So, you guys are inside the costume, and I'm the delivery man," JJ informs.

"Cool, this just might work!" Calvin responds. Brad flashes a big smile and chuckles.

"Wait, wait, I'm going to be inside an elephant costume with Calvin? You're kidding me!" Brad says while still laughing.

"Yeah, and right before the zoo closes, we show up," JJ adds as Calvin nods.

"Surprise! What can they say? Every baby needs its mama," Calvin proclaims.

"That's right. Then once they take the baby to Big Mama, I'll find the main gate used for the animals. And when the time is right, I'll contact you guys using Calvin's walkie-talkie," JJ informs.

"The escape!" excited Calvin declares.

"Yep, we'll travel at night. When we get back to the neighborhood, we'll hide in the desert and hopefully wait for the Magical Storm!" JJ concludes as Brad sports a puzzled expression.

"Dude, when does all of this happen?" a curious Brad asks. JJ gives Brad and Calvin a serious look.

"Tonight. We got to act fast. This place is going to be crawling with people. Besides, who knows where Big Mama could be taken to?" JJ says. The boys all sport determined expressions and share nods.

"Well then, let's go buy some shag rugs and paint," Calvin announces.

"My mom is at work. We can make the costumes at my house," Brad adds as the boys share smile and high-five one another.

It's later in the day, and the boys are staring at two piles of black shag rug material spread out on some newspaper in a typical two-car garage floor. Next to the piles are several empty cans of black spray paint. JJ gives Calvin and Brad an encouraging smile.

"Well, let's see what it looks like," JJ announces. Immediately, Calvin and Brad lock in with squinted eyes and quickly get into their gun draw position. They both know the stakes are high, and the moment is tense because the loser will be the back half of the costume. Calvin knows the consequences of losing and decides to start the count down.

"On three," a determined Calvin states as the boys' squinted eyes get even tighter.

"One, two, three," they call out together.

"Rock, paper, scissors…Shoot!" they blast out.

A split second later, the boys draw hands with Calvin drawing paper and Brad throwing scissors. Brad gets wide-eyed and quickly reacts with victory fist pumps into the air.

"Hello to the winner and the new head of the fake baby mammoth costume…Yours truly!" Brad yells out, rubbing it into Calvin, who is exceptionally annoyed and looking very upset. He gives Brad a stern look while shaking his pointed finger at him.

"I'm warning you now, Thompson!" an angry Calvin proclaims as Brad half grins, trying to act innocent.

"What? I don't get it," a sheepish Brad says, pretending he is clueless.

"You know what I mean. You'll eat anything, and your afterburners are terrible!" an annoyed Calvin replies. Brad gives JJ a dumbfounded glance with a slight smirk as he still acts like he does not know what Calvin is upset about. JJ looks at Brad with raised eyebrow and gives him the "Yeah, right" face as he shakes his head.

"Come on, guys, let's check it out," an eager JJ says.

A short while later, JJ is holding one of the walkie-talkies in his hand and is standing next to a rag doll of a baby mammoth costume on all fours. The fake baby mammoth has a short black stubby trunk, floppy ears, a short tail, but unnoticed during construction, there are no eyes. An internal description would reveal Brad's head inside the head of the costume. He is bent over about forth-five degrees with his right arm inside the trunk. His legs are extended down into the front two legs of the baby mammoth costume. Calvin is bent over with the right side of his head resting on Brad's lower back. He is wearing a walkie-talkie headset, and his legs extend down into the two rear legs. Calvin is quite aggravated and is not in a good mood by any means.

JJ brings the walkie-talkie to his mouth and is anxious to fine-tune operations.

"Testing…one, two, three…Can you hear me?" JJ asks as the rear of the costume shimmies back and forth.

"Like yeah! You're standing right next to me!" states Calvin, who is still highly annoyed.

"Dude, it's really hot in here, and my stomach is starting to growl," Brad announces from the front half.

"Man, I don't want to hear that!" a perturbed Calvin yells out. "This is no time to be the funny man!"

"No, I'm not joking. My stomach is really aching," Brad replies.

"Geez, JJ…What's next?" an agitated Calvin asks. JJ sports a slight smile and shakes his head.

"Look, guys, we need to practice walking, and you'll have to learn to coordinate your steps," JJ informs.

"Yeah, yeah…fine!" Calvin promptly responds. The fake baby mammoth starts to shake its head and lets out a squeaky roar.

"Cut it out, Brad, and you lead! It's your left and my right, your right, and my left…Got it!" Calvin aggressively instructs.

"That's kind of complicated, but I think I got," Brad responds. The fake baby mammoth starts to nudge forward as JJ curiously watches. Slowly, the front left leg moves forward, and simultaneously the back right leg follows.

"Keep it steady," JJ encouragingly says. But after a couple of steps, Brad repeats the left leg move and follows with another left leg and not the right. It does not take long before the mammoth is out of balance and falls on its right side with a thud. JJ haplessly watches the ragged costume lying on its right side as the left legs are kicking back and forth. JJ flashes a half grin and just shakes his head.

"Brad, man, we need to alternate steps. Got it!" a frustrated Calvin calls out.

"Got confused, sorry," Brad responds. JJ helps the boys, who are still in the fake baby mammoth costume, get back on their feet. Inside, Calvin is grumbling as Brad grunts and groans.

"All right, one more time," JJ instructs. Moments later the fake baby mammoth is walking circles around JJ. He sports a smile and brings the walkie-talkie to his mouth.

"Good enough, fellas. I think you got it!" an optimistic JJ states as he walks over to the mammoth and lifts a piece of costume in the center of the back. Then he pulls on a drawstring, causing the costume to separate in half at the center. Immediately, Clavin stands straight up as he holds his half of the costume at his waist, looking very annoyed. Brad promptly takes the head of the costume off and gives JJ an urgent look.

"Whew, it's hot in there," Brad announces as Calvin flashes a smirky grin.

"You don't say," a perturb Calvin replies. JJ gives his friends an encouraging smile, then sports a serious face.

"We roll tonight," JJ reminds the two as Calvin and Brad share an apprehensive glance.

"We'll tell our parents we're having a sleepover and take the late afternoon bus to the zoo," JJ adds. "We'll hang out till it's time." JJ gives his friends the thumbs-up as Calvin and Brad nod.

It is late evening but getting dark fast. A light shine over an arched sign above the visitor entrance gate that reads, "Welcome to The Phoenix Zoo."

JJ slyly peeks around some bushes. He is dressed in one of Calvin's Eagle Scout uniforms and wears a piece of the black shag rug as a mustache to look older. Along with his outfit, he holds a clipboard in one hand and a pen in the other with a walkie-talkie tuck in his back pocket. Behind JJ, Calvin and Brad are anxiously holding their costume halves, waiting for their moment.

"Looks like the last group of visitors are leaving," JJ informs Calvin and Brad, who share an eager glance.

At the gate, a family of four—a man, a woman, a young boy, and a girl—are walking through the gate entrance. Next to them, an older man wearing green pants and matching shirt waves goodbye as he closes the gate and locks it shut.

Back at the bushes, JJ's eyes are squinted and are moving side-to-side as he studies the surroundings. He focuses on the gate and the tall zoo fence that extends twenty yards in both directions. The fence blends into plants, bushes, and an assortment of medium-length trees. In the background throughout the zoo, Mexican palm trees dot the grounds with light poles neatly spaced along the zoo walkways. Then one-by-one, most of the light poles start to shut off, leaving the zoo dimly lit with the remaining half-dozen light poles scattered throughout the property.

JJ turns around and gives Calvin and Brad a serious look while half of his mustache hangs over his lip.

"Time to rock!" a pumped JJ says as Calvin and Brad give JJ a smile. Brad points to JJ's mustache. JJ gets cross-eyed as he looks down toward his lip and quickly pushes the piece of shag rug back in place. Brad continues to hold his smile.

"Dude, that mustache looks good on you. Makes you look older. What do you think, Calvin?" Brad asks. Calvin rolls his eyes and shakes his head.

"Man, let's just put the costume on!" an irritated Calvin responds. So, the boys get busy and prepare for their next move.

A few minutes later, JJ's is standing in front of the main gate holding the clipboard and looking as official as possible. Next to him Calvin and Brad are in the fake baby mammoth costume, waiting for instructions with a slight grumbling sound coming from the back half.

"Okay, get ready, and be quiet!" JJ mutters as he starts to knock on the gate door.

"Hello!" JJ yells out. "We have a special delivery! Anyone home?" After about thirty seconds, the gate light suddenly comes on, and the sound of faint footsteps gets louder and louder. JJ looks down at the fake baby mammoth.

"Okay, guys, stay calm. Somebody is coming," JJ announces. From inside the costume, Brad lets out a tiny roar.

"Cut it out, Brad!" Calvin responds. JJ gives the mammoth a nudge with his hip.

"Quiet!" JJ says. "Here comes the zookeeper."

Walking up to the gate is the zookeeper with the name "Bob" on a tag pinned to his green work shirt. He appears in his late sixties and wears a green baseball cap that matches the rest of his outfit.

"Well, well, well, and what do we have here?" Bob says as he greets JJ. He looks up at Bob, who has not seen the fake baby mammoth standing behind JJ at this point.

"Good evening, sir, we have the new mammoth's baby," JJ informs the zookeeper as he steps aside to reveal the surprise. Bob takes a second look and flashes a puzzled expression.

"Baby! I didn't hear any news about a baby mammoth," Bob responds.

"Yes, sir, in all the commotion, they forgot to bring the baby. And she is starved!" JJ proclaims. Bob looks dumbfounded and rubs his chin.

"Well, it's too late to call Dr. Charles. So best get the baby with her mother, at least for the night," Bob says as JJ flashes a big smile.

"Good idea," a relieved JJ replies. Bob opens the gate and walks out toward JJ and the fake baby mammoth. Then Bob gives the baby mammoth a suspicious look as he bends over for a better view. JJ appears apprehensive as Bod stands straight up and gives JJ a questionable look.

"That's strange. The baby has no eyes," Bob says. JJ gets wide-eyed and is caught off guard as he rears his head back and looks at the costume head. He shakes his head and takes another look.

"Ahh…well, the baby's so new. She hasn't opened her eyes yet…and she really needs her mom," a nervous JJ responds. Bob shrugs and nods.

"Makes sense. Well, follow me," Bob says, and just as he turns around, JJ's mustache falls halfway off again. But JJ quickly reacts and fixes the mustache as he walks the baby through the gate, following Bob.

"This way," Bob states as he turns his head around and sees JJ holding up the back of the costume. Inside the disguise, Calvin and Brad are having difficulty coordinating their steps and are stumbling along. JJ sees Bob curiously looking at him.

"It's still having a hard time walking," JJ quickly responds with a smile. Bob turns his head around and resumes his walk.

"No eyes and can barely walk…poor little thing," Bob mutters to himself.

A couple of minutes later, Bob is standing in front of a large iron gate to the elephant cage that holds Big Mama. JJ and the baby are standing directly behind him. JJ is eager to get the boys inside the cage. Bob starts to slide a bolt to open the gate when he suddenly stops and slams the bolt back in place. He turns around and gives JJ a stern look.

"If you don't mind, I'd like to call Dr. Freeman's secretary. You can wait right here," Bob abruptly says. He quickly walks away, leaving JJ looking bewildered.

"JJ, what's going on? I can tell he left," a curious Calvin

says. Suddenly, Brad groans.

"Hey, you guys, I don't feel so good," Brad mutters out loud. JJ quickly grabs the walkie-talkie and brings it to his mouth as his eyes scan the surroundings.

"I don't know. It sounds like he wants to talk to a… Dr. Freeman," JJ responds as he continues to look around.

"What should we do?" a quizzical Calvin asks.

"Just be quiet and stand still. I'm going to make sure all the cage doors are unlocked. And besides, there's got to be a bigger entrance gate somewhere for the larger animals. Just stay calm. I'll be right back," JJ says as he quickly walks away. He knows time is of the essence, and he must have an exit plan for the escape to be successful. Any delays could be a disaster. Meanwhile, the situation inside the costume is about to take a turn for the worse, especially for Calvin.

"Calvin, I'm not kidding, I feel sick," Brad mutters from the front of the costume.

"Will you just stop?" an annoyed Calvin replies.

The fake baby mammoth is standing alone by itself in front of the gate when suddenly, it happens—Brad lets loose a loud and nasty gastral explosion of immense portions.

"Oh, come on, man!" Calvin cries out. "You are sick and disgusting!"

"Sorry," a sheepish Brad responds as Calvin gags and dry heaves.

JJ returns from scouting the area. As he walks up to the fake baby mammoth and leans over to talk to Calvin and

Brad, he catches a whiff, causing his face to cringe.

"Ugh!" JJ mutters. "What happened in there?" Calvin tries to answer but is still gagging and struggling with the smell.

"JJ, I need help in here!" a desperate Calvin says. Suddenly, JJ hears approaching footsteps.

"Quiet!" JJ commands. "The zookeeper is coming back!" Bob walks up to JJ as he stares at the ground, shaking his head.

"Why do I have to be here bright and early?" Bob grumbles to himself as he looks at JJ. "Well, something big is going on in the lab, and we're not to bother Dr. Freeman, so in the cage she goes," Bob says. He slides the bolt lock and pushes the gate open. Inside the cage Big Mama stands with her head down in the corner, looking depressed. Bob walks into the cage and holds the door open.

"Okay, bring her in," Bob says. JJ walks in the cage with the fake baby mammoth, and as they walk past Bob, he takes a couple of sniffs and immediately flashes a sour face.

"Boy, it's not only ugly, but stinky too." Bob mutters to himself.

JJ guides the fake baby mammoth to the center of the cage as Big Mama keeps her head down in the corner.

"That should do it," JJ tells the zookeeper but loud enough for Calvin and Brad to have an idea of where they are. But Big Mama hears JJ's voice and gets wide-eyed, and she turns her head to see JJ. Meanwhile, JJ hands Bob the clipboard and the pen. Bob signs a paper and hands the clipboard along with the pen back to JJ.

"Thank you," JJ says. He then walks out of the cage, followed by Bob. Bob stops and turns around to lock the gate door. JJ intently watches as Bob slides the bolt shut, knowing he must keep the door unlocked. As they walk away, JJ abruptly stops and gives Bob a serious look.

"I forgot to do a last visual inspection, and can I just look through the cage door to make it official…if that's okay with you?" JJ asks. "I'll meet you at the main entrance." Bob looks a little perturbed but nods.

"Sure," he responds as he begins to walk toward the main entrance gate. JJ calmly walks to the cage door and quietly slides the bolt open, then walks away.

Inside the cage a curious Big Mama walks over to the fake baby mammoth. She looks suspicious and takes a sniff. The creature's eyes cringe as she pulls back her head and lets out a grunt.

Outside the zoo JJ is crouched down next to some bushes close to the main entrance gate. He watches Bob get into an older model pickup truck and soon rumbles away. JJ brings the walkie-talkie to his mouth.

"Hey, Calvin, can you read me?" JJ asks.

"JJ, I got to get out of this thing! Brad's making me sick!" a desperate Calvin responds.

"Look, the coast is clear. I unlocked the gate door and the main gate. Get Big Mama out of there and meet me at the entrance!" JJ informs.

"That's great news because I thought I was going to die!" a jubilant Calvin replies.

The fake baby mammoth is standing still inside the cage as Big Mama suspiciously eyes the strange-looking little creature. Suddenly, the costume quickly separates in the middle with Calvin popping up and taking a big gasp of air. He looks exhilarated as Brad stands there with the costume head still on.

"Man, you need to see a doctor!" Calvin calls out. Brad still has the costume head on, then promptly takes it off, giving Calvin an innocent look.

"Dude, I said I'm sorry," Brad humbly replies. Big Mama walks up to the two boys and rubs her trunk against the top of their heads. Her eyes gleam as she lets out a friendly roar while Calvin and Brad share a laugh.

"Let's get out of these rags. We need to meet JJ at the main entrance gate!" Calvin anxiously announces.

JJ eagerly awaits outside the gate as he methodically scans the area. He gets wide-eyed at the sound of footsteps as the ground starts to vibrate. Suddenly, out of the dim light, Calvin and Brad rush up to the gate with Big Mama directly behind them. Soon, the three boys gather as Big Mama sticks her trunk through the gate and gives JJ a gentle nudge.

"Wow, you guys did it!" JJ enthusiastically says. Calvin gives JJ a half grin.

"It wasn't without sacrifice," Calvin responds as he gives Brad a wry look. Then JJ looks up to Big Mama.

"Hey, Big Mama, we're going to get you back to your baby," JJ proclaims as Calvin sizes up the entrance gate and gives JJ a puzzled expression.

"JJ, we'll never get Big Mama through this gate!" an alarmed Calvin declares. JJ sports a confident smile and points toward his right.

"I've already checked it out. There's a big animal gate next to the golf course. Follow me," JJ informs as he streaks off. Calvin and Brad toss their costumes to the ground and quickly dash off, with Big Mama following.

A few minutes later, JJ is holding a flashlight as he stands outside a huge iron bar gate located in the back of the zoo. It's a two-section gate, each ten feet long, designed to open and allow large animals such as elephants to enter the grounds. The flashlight beam reflects off a large steel chain that connects the two gates together and is locked from the inside for security reasons. The three boys look perplexed as they stare at the chain.

"This chain is huge!" an anxious Calvin says. Brad picks up a large stick from the ground and wedges it inside the chain lock.

"Here, let me try," Brad says as he tries to pry the chain lock open. He grunts and groans, exerting his strength, but the lock doesn't budge. Brad sports a determined look and tries one more blast of strength, when suddenly, the stick breaks with a loud *snap*, sending Brad falling to the ground on his butt. The boys share a helpless glance.

"Now what?" Brad asks while Calvin can only shrug. Meanwhile, JJ is staring off in deep thought when suddenly, he gets wide-eyed and looks up at Big Mama.

"I got an idea!" JJ eagerly announces. He reaches his hand through the cage gate and grabs Big Mama's trunk, then he guides the snout to the chain link and looks up at Big Mama.

"Big Mama, we need some muscle. Pull this chain apart for us," JJ asks the huge beast. Big Mama understands and quickly wraps her snout around the chain. In a matter of seconds, she gives the chain a powerful tug, snapping it into two. She tosses the chain to the ground as the boys look on with ecstatic faces.

"Open the gate, and let's get out of here!" JJ enthusiastically instructs as the boys share a smile.

"Yeah, the escape!" Calvin calls out. Brad flashes a puzzled look.

"Where are we headed?" a curious Brad asks. JJ aims the flashlight toward the darkness.

"To the golf course," JJ responds.

About fifteen minutes later, under the dark night of a quarter moon, the boys are kneeling in a tight circle on the par five number thirteen tee box of a public golf course. Brad is holding the flashlight while JJ searches in Calvin's backpack and suddenly pulls out another flashlight. JJ hands the flashlight to Calvin, then sports a serious face.

"Okay, gives us three quick flashes, and we'll follow the light," JJ instructs as Calvin nods.

"Got it. Through the golf course, along the irrigation canal, and across the interstate," Calvin replies.

"Yeah, then down the runoff canal and hideout in the desert," Brad adds. The boys share a smile and stand up together, ready for their mission. The plan sounds simple, but the boys know they have several miles to travel and a lot of work to do before the morning light makes everything more difficult, if not impossible.

Calvin glances out into the darkness, then back to JJ and Brad.

"I'll keep in touch with the walkie-talkie, but we need to keep it quiet," Calvin says as he starts to walk away.

The flashlight beam bounces on the ground in front of Calvin as JJ and Brad watch him disappear into the night. JJ brings the walkie-talkie to his mouth.

"Good luck. Over," JJ softly mutters as Brad and he share a glance, then stare out toward the dark fairway with only the faint light of the moon dancing off the tops of the Mexican palm trees that line the number thirteen challenge. Suddenly, three quick flashes of light appear about five hundred yards away. JJ points out toward the signal.

"That's Calvin!" an anxious JJ states as he brings the walkie-talkie to his mouth.

"We're on our way. Over," a reassuring JJ says. A second later, JJ's walkie-talkie crackles.

"Hurry up, guys. It's scary out here," a nervous Calvin replies. Then out of the pitch-black end of the tee box, Brad leads Big Mama by a rope tied to her tusk. Together, they walk up to JJ.

"Big Mama's ready," Brad announces. JJ pets the animal's trunk as he sports a smile.

"Follow me," JJ says as he walks off the tee box. He looks up at the moonlight and sees a cloud passing through and blocking what little light the moon gives. But for JJ and the boys, that's a good thing because they need all the cover they can get.

A few minutes later, under a dark sky, Brad and Big Mama are walking together, while JJ leads the way with the flashlight about twenty yards ahead. JJ carefully guides Brad and Big Mama as the beam of light dances around the ground. As they cautiously move toward Calvin's location, the huge woolly's foot sinks several inches into the lush grass with each step. Brad takes a quick glance at the foot impression and gets wide-eyed.

"Boy, there's going to be some new hazards on this hole," Brad mutters to himself.

JJ continues to walk down the fairway, scanning his way with the flashlight. The beam of light sweeps back and forth, revealing a small sand bunker just off to his left, almost in the center of the fairway. A few yards from the bunker and lying close to his path, JJ spots a rake in the grass. He turns his head to give Brad a warning.

"Hey, Brad, look out for this rake," JJ informs as Brad flashes a quizzical expression.

"What?" Brad asks, when suddenly, he steps on the rake, sending the handle straight up and whacking him in the face. The force knocks him to the ground on his butt.

"Ugh! Ouch!" Brad yells out.

"Hey, quiet down!" JJ responds. Brad slowly gets up, looking perturbed as he adjusts his Cubs hat.

"Great. What else can happen in the middle of nowhere?" a sarcastic Brad wonders out loud. But no sooner does he say that than a suspicious sound of a metal click is heard nearby. He sports a curious look when suddenly, a blast of water from the fairway sprinkler system hits Brad right in the face.

"Geez!" Brad calls out as Big Mama lets out a roar. JJ quickly turns around with the flashlight.

"Hey, keep it down, and follow me!" JJ commands.

At the number fourteen tee box, a nervous Calvin flashes a look of concern as he reaches for his walkie-talkie and adjusts the mouthpiece.

"JJ, what's with all the racket?" an anxious Calvin asks.

"Oh…nothing. We'll be right there," JJ responds through the walkie-talkie. Calvin shakes his head when a moment later, the bushes behind him at the tee box start to rustle.

"Well, it's about time," Calvin mutters to himself. The rustling gets louder, then unexpectedly, Calvin hears growling. He gets wide-eyed and looks concerned, realizing the sound is not JJ and company. His apprehension grows as the growling gets louder and more numerous.

"Oh no, better move slow," Calvin says as he slowly

turns around with the flashlight. The beam runs across some bushes when it abruptly shines on a pack of five angry-eyed coyotes. Quickly, the beam of light centers on the coyotes' juicy, drooling mouths with big canine teeth. Slowly, the creatures creep towards Calvin, who is petrified in fear. He cautiously reaches down with his shaking hand and pushes the "Speak" button of the walkie-talkie clipped to his hip.

"JJ…help. There's a pack of coyotes licking their chops!" a frightened Calvin says with a gulp.

"Hang in there, Calvin. We're almost there," JJ replies. Fear stretches Calvin's face when he sees the largest of the animals emerge from the center of the pack and steadily move closer. The animal's shoulders are hunched, and with a mouth full of teeth, it's ready to leap. A spilt second later, the coyote attacks, jumping straight at Calvin. The huge teeth and drooling mouth are just inches away from Calvin's face. His eyes are tightly closed in panic as he feels the warm drool splat on his chick. Then suddenly, there's a loud *thump* as the coyote sails away into the darkness. Standing over Calvin is Big Mama, who whips her trunk through the air as she lets out a thunderous roar. Calvin immediately turns around and, with much relief, flashes a beam of light on the mammoth's head. She whips her trunk around again, letting out another intimidating roar. The four other coyotes want no part of the giant beast, their eyes widening and their jaws dropping. In terror, they quickly scamper away with their tails between their legs, disappearing into the darkness. Seconds later the boys gather next to Big Mama and share a smile.

"Just in time!" a joyful Calvin calls out.

"I'll say you were about to become a doggie treat," Brad responds as the boys share a chuckle. JJ looks out toward the nearby irrigation canal, then gives Calvin and Brad a serious look.

"Let's roll. We don't have much time," JJ announces as he leads the way off the tee box.

About a half hour later and under the dull, dark light of the moon, the three boys lead Big Mama down a bike path that is next to a fifteen-yard-wide irrigation canal filled with water. Directly on the other side of the canal is a maintenance road with light poles about every fifty yards. The night is calm as the faint moonlight reflects off the gentle flow of the water.

Time is essential as the boys walk side-by-side down the bike path. They know they have a long way to go and must cross the interstate that's miles away while it's still dark. Brad holds the rope that leads Big Mama, who smoothly struts behind them. Brad gives JJ a curious look.

"So, JJ, whose house did you tell your parents you were spending the night?" a curious Brad asks.

"Calvin's…Why?" JJ replies as Brad flashes a skeptical expression.

"Hmm, I told my mom I'm staying at your house," Brad informs. Calvin gives the two boys a dubious look.

"That's great. I'm supposed to be at Brad's house!" Calvin responds. Brad flashes a grin.

"Busted!" Brad announces as the boys continue their mission.

After about a half hour later, the group is near a large boulder formation surrounded by bushes and trees. The back side of the boulders disappears in the darkness. Suddenly, JJ gets wide-eyed.

"Look, a patrol car!" an anxious JJ alerts.

Under a streetlight about fifty yards ahead across the channel, a police car slowly cruises on a maintenance road. The vehicle's lights are off, and it's heading straight toward the group's location.

The boys are totally caught off guard and look surprised. Fortunately, they're near the group of boulders that catches JJ's eyes.

"Hey, check it out, it looks like a cave or something!" an excited JJ says. Calvin and Brad look toward the boulders and share a nod.

"Our options are limited," Calvin proclaims.

"We better hide!" JJ states as Brad leads Big Mama through a row of bushes, revealing a huge opening in the boulders. The entrance is like a cave, but it's not too deep. The group scuffles through the bushes and vanishes into the darkness of the entrance.

Directly across the channel, the police vehicle continues to slowly edge down the maintenance road. The driver's window is down as the officer scans the area.

The boys are nervous and wide-eyed as together their heads turn in the pitch blackness, following the vehicle. Brad suspiciously looks around.

"Dude, it's sure dark in here!" an anxious Brad states. Then he turns on the flashlight, and within a split second, the cave is full of bats flying wildly in all directions. The boys, along with Big Mama, freak out as they are consumed with thousands of flying bats. The multitude of high-pitched squeaking and the constant flapping of the wings fill the cave entrance area. Bats are darting and whirling all around the boys and Big Mama. Brad is aggressively waving his arms as JJ swats the air with his hat. The scene is frightening and chaotic.

"Ahh!" Brad screams out as Calvin frantically brushes his hair.

"JJ, I've got a bat stuck in my hair! Do something!" Calvin cries out. JJ quickly starts to swat Calvin's head with his hat.

"Geez, we got to get out of here!" JJ yells out. Then suddenly, from behind the boys, Big Mama goes into the panic mode and starts to shake her head and whip her trunk in all directions. In her fright she lets out a thunderous roar.

Across the channel the officer is sipping a cup of coffee when he hears a roar in the night. He gets curiously wide-eyed and turns his head toward the noise across the channel. Then he puts down the cup of coffee and picks up the mic. Abruptly, he puts the mic down and puts the vehicle in reverse as he starts to shine his spotlight toward the group's location.

On the other side of the channel, the boys and Big Mama are edgy as they stare out at the police vehicle. Big Mama is so tall that half her head is exposed as the beam of light moves across the boulders heading in her direction. Then the beam of light moves in front of the bushes that hide the boys. They quickly crouch down as they share an anxious glance.

In the police vehicle, the officer picks up the mic and holds it to his mouth. His eyes are tense as he looks across the channel with his thumb on the speaker button, ready to report to headquarters. Then surprisingly, he lowers the mic, flashing a big smile as he nods.

"Ah…zoo noises," the officer mutters out to himself. He reattaches the mic to the holder as the vehicle drives away, disappearing in the darkness between light poles.

Behind the bushes the boys let out a collective sigh of relief as they watch the vehicle pull away.

"Man, that was close!" Calvin proclaims as Brad aggressively brushes himself off, while JJ keeps a sharp eye in the direction of the police vehicle.

"Dudes, that was super freaky!" Brad states as he brushes his legs. "You don't see any bats on me, do you?" JJ gives Brad a quick glance.

"No, you're bat-free," JJ informs Brad. "Let's go. We got to get to the interstate." The boys share a nod and resume their journey.

Chapter Eleven

TO THE DESERT AND BEYOND

After a couple of hours, the boys are peeking out from behind some bushes at the base of a billboard. They diligently scan the two-way street that runs over the interstate, knowing that their next move needs to be perfectly executed. The interstate bridge is lined with light poles, then fades into darkness that is near their destination. Behind them, there is more darkness except on the eastern horizon, where evidence of a faint predawn sunrise begins to silhouette Superstition Mountain. The boys continue to scan the bridge.

"We got to get across the bridge before the morning traffic!" an anxious Calvin says.

"I'll set up a roadblock across the bridge. When the coast is clear, I'll let you know, and you'll need to hustle Big Mama across," JJ informs. Calvin and Brad nod in agreement as the three boys disappear behind the bushes.

Meanwhile, back at the zoo, Bob has reported to work extra early as requested. He unlocks the main gate and causally looks toward the ground. He squints in a curious fashion as he stares at the two piles of the black shaggy costume.

"Hmm…what's this?" a puzzled Bod mutters to himself. He picks up one of the piles and examines it closely.

"That's interesting. No eyes," Bob states. Then he flashes a confused expression and takes a double look. "No eyes!" a shaken Bob dashes away.

JJ has positioned himself on the other side of the bridge and has gathered several large mesquite branches downed by the storm in the center of the street as a roadblock. Soon, a vehicle approaches, and he signals the car to stop with his flashlight. The older model Ford pulls up to JJ as the driver's side window rolls down. JJ flashes a friendly smile as he leans in toward the window.

"Good morning, sir. We have got a little problem here, but if you take the next street north, you can get to the interstate," JJ calmly instructs.

"Thanks, kid," the driver responds. The car backs up and turns around and heads north. JJ watches the vehicle pull away and brings the walkie-talkie to his mouth.

"Calvin, here's our chance! Hurry up!" an eager JJ says.

Behind the billboard, Calvin and Brad have been anxiously waiting to hear from JJ. Calvin flashes a smile of relief and adjusts his mouthpiece.

"Okay," Calvin quickly replies. He scans the surrounding area and notices four road barricades making a square over a hole in the street located near their location. He turns to Brad.

"Brad, take Big Mama over the bridge. JJ will be waiting, and I'll be right there," Calvin says as he dashes toward the barricades. Brad then leads Big Mama around the billboard.

"Come on, Big Mama, we're going for a jog," Brad tells his big friend.

Meanwhile, Calvin starts placing the barricades next to each other, neatly blocking the street that leads to the bridge. Suddenly, he stares down the road and sees a car's headlights gaining ground in his direction. He takes a quick look toward the bridge and back to the headlights while sporting a concerned look.

"I better wait and see," Calvin mutters to himself as he stands next to the barricade.

On the bridge over the interstate, a homeless man sits on the ground, leaning up against the security fence. He has long scraggly black hair with a beard and patiently waits for the morning traffic while holding a bagged bottle in one hand and a sign that reads, "Need Money for Food" in the other hand. While sitting, he curiously turns his head toward the other end of the road when he hears loud thumping of heavy footsteps. Suddenly, to his surprise, he sees Brad leading Big Mama by a rope crossing the bridge coming directly to his location. The homeless man is bewildered and startled by the sight of the giant beast. Brad looks at the homeless fellow and flashes a big smile.

"The circus is in town! Grab a shovel!" Brad says in jest. The homeless man can't believe his eyes and quickly tosses the bagged bottle, then rips his sign in half.

"I need to find a new bridge," he mutters to himself.

Back at the zoo, Bob is inside the elephant cage holding the fake baby mammoth costume. He's drop-jawed and beside himself at the sight of the empty cage.

"I thought that baby mammoth looked strange," Bob proclaims as he throws the costume to the ground. "I got to notify Dr. Charles!" a frustrated Bob says as he picks up the costume and dashes off.

Across the interstate bridge, Brad and Big Mama jog up to JJ. The two boys slap a high five and share a smile.

"Great work, Brad!" an enthusiastic JJ says. "Where's Calvin?" Brad takes a couple of deep breaths and looks toward the bridge.

"I don't know. He was going to do something and then catch up with us," Brad responds. JJ nods and points to the drainage canal.

"Well, let's get down to the drainage canal and hide Big Mama before sunrise," JJ says.

Back at the barricade, Calvin nervously watches the car's headlight get closer. Then just a couple of blocks away, the vehicle turns, and the headlights are gone.

"Good," a relieved Calvin says. Suddenly, from behind Calvin, a hand grabs his headpiece and rips it off his head. Calvin looks startled and quickly turns around. Directly in front of him are three men dressed in black jeans and black leather vests, all looking like street bullies. There are two big guys wearing sunglasses standing alongside the apparent leader of the group. He's slightly taller than Calvin and gives him a harsh look as he steps forward.

"What's in the backpack, pal?" the leader asks. Calvin is taken by surprise and looks frightened.

"Ah…nothing, really, just a bunch of stuff," Calvin replies as the leader steps closer.

"Oh yeah, so you say," the leader responds in a sharp tone. Then he turns away but quickly turns around toward Calvin and punches him in the stomach. Calvin doubles over in pain and tries to catch his breath. He realizes the moment is tense and slightly turns to his right, keeping his walkie-talkie clipped to his belt out of view from the assailants. Cleverly, he starts to tap out the SOS code on the talk button. Calvin moans, buying time to tap the button quickly three times, then repeats the three taps at a slower pace. He moans again and follows with three quick taps.

At the drainage canal, JJ is petting Big Mama's trunk, keeping the huge animal as calm as possible, while Brad nonchalantly places mesquite branches throughout her woolly side to camouflage their big friend. The drainage canal serves as a good hiding spot with its walls about eight feet high and width close to fifteen feet. Because of the history of water running off into the desert, there's plenty of bushes and other vegetation serving as good cover to hide.

Suddenly, JJ sports a curious expression as the sound of taps comes through his walkie-talkie. He abruptly grabs the walkie-talkie from his belt and gives the device a serious look as the tapping continues.

"Hmm…dit, dit, dits, then slow dah, dah dahs, and quicker dit, dit, dits," a puzzled JJ mutters to himself. "Now where have I heard that before, and why is it coming through the walkie-talkie?" a curious JJ asks. Then he gets wide-eyed, realizing the code. "Wait, that's the SOS distress code! Calvin's in trouble!" an alarmed JJ yells out. Brad immediately stops placing the mesquite branches on Big Mama and flashes a serious look.

"Calvin…in trouble. Wait here!" Brad responds as he dashes off and sprints back toward the bridge.

Meanwhile, at the barricade, things are looking grim as the three bullies are standing directly in front of Calvin. To the leader's right, bully number one is tapping a baseball bat as intimidatingly as possible into his hand. To Calvin's right or left of the leader, bully number two is waiting his turn.

"Hand over the backpack, or my friend here will crack your skull open," the leader demands. Calvin slowly stands back up straight, his eyes cringed in pain as he gasps for breath.

"Sure, Mister," Calvin mutters out. He slips off the backpack and hands it over. The leader rips it out of Calvin's hand.

"Good," the leader says with a sinister chuckle. "My friend is still going to bust your head." Bully number one draws back the baseball bat and is ready to swing when suddenly, Brad's hand grabs the bully's wrist with one hand and his elbow with the other. When Calvin is messed with, it means messing with Brad too, and he is not going to waste time when he needs to defend his best friend. He holds the elbow firm as he pushes the wrist backward. The bully cringes in pain as the sound of grinding bones and twisted tendons fills the air. Brad continues to push the wrist backward and downward, quickly taking the thug to the ground. Bully number one grabs his shoulder, moaning and groaning in pain as Brad has rendered him helpless. Bully number two flashes a mean, threatening look as he steps closer to Brad.

"Okay, Mr. Tough Guy Hero!" bully number two calls out. Then he swings a right punch at Brad. The air whooshes as Brad pulls his head back, avoiding the punch.

"Ugh…take this!" the bully yells as he throws a left punch, but Brad quickly dodges the attack. In a flash Brad counters with a shocking right roundhouse kick to the bully's thigh. He yells out in pain and grabs his leg. He gives Brad an evil look as he pulls out some brass knuckles out of his pocket and slips them on his right hand. The bully gives Brad the look of death.

"You're finished, punk!" bully number two belts out. He lunges at Brad, taking a mighty swing, but Brad smoothly steps back and avoids any contact. Brad wastes no time to respond and takes a step forward before conducting a jump spin to his right, delivering a devastating 360-degree aerial roundhouse kick. It's a graceful move as Brad's right foot smashes into the right jaw of the assailant, dropping him to the ground moaning.

The leader looks at Brad, and then his eyes quickly catch a broken glass bottle on the street, much like a soda bottle. He then grabs the neck of the bottle with his right hand pointing the sharp edges toward Brad. He tosses the backpack to the ground with his left hand and gives Brad a curious look.

"Who are you, kid?" the leader questions as Brad calmly gets into his martial arts position and stares down the leader.

"Your mistake of the night," Brad responds, taking a quick glance at Calvin. "Get your backpack, Calvin." Calvin promptly picks up his backpack and makes a quick body gesture toward the leader, then he steps aside. The main bully moves side-to-side, aiming the sharp, pointed glass tips at Brad.

"Let's see what you got," the leader says as he quickly lunges the bottle at Brad, who immediately jumps back, avoiding the strike.

"The problem here is, my friend and I don't have the time to really get to know you, guys," Brad calmly says. The leader gives Brad a puzzled look at the statement, then squints before lunging the bottle at Brad for the second time. But Brad responds with a blazingly fast left-to-right midsection leg sweep, knocking the glass bottle out of the bully's hand. The main attacker blankly glances down at his empty hand, then without hesitation, Brad conducts another lightning quick move with a lower right-to-left leg sweep, dropping the leader hard to the ground. He looks up at Brad with his hands up.

"Okay, enough!" the leader cries out. Brad just stares at him as he gets back into his martial arts position and steps closer to the bully with his fist ready at his hip.

"I'll decide that." Brad replies as he takes another step forward. Calvin quickly grabs Brad by the shoulder.

"Hey, JJ's waiting," Calvin states. Brad nods while looking at the two big bullies on the ground, shaking his head and pointing his finger at them. He looks at the leader and gives him a two-finger eye gesture like "I'm watching you," then points his index finger at him.

"Later," Brad informs. The two boys dash off and sprint toward the bridge. As the two are running, Calvin gives Brad a glance.

"Thanks," Calvin says. Brad sports a smile and lays his hand out. Calvin returns the smile and gives Brad a soft hand slap.

The faint morning light has begun to reveal itself over the

city. At the zoo, Dr. Charles is sitting at the desk diligently reviewing some paperwork under his study lamp. Suddenly, there's loud, aggressive knocking on the office door. He curiously looks at his watch and then looks toward the door.

"Come in," Dr. Charles says. The door flies open and slams against the wall as Bob rushes to the office.

"Dr. Charles!" an anxious Bob cries out. Dr. Charles puts down some research paper and gives Bob a friendly smile.

"Well, good morning, Bob. And what can I do for you this lovely start of the day?" Dr. Charles asks. Bob is trembling as he holds the two costume halves, one in each hand, as he gives Dr. Charles a desperate look.

"Dr. Charles, I don't know how to tell you this, but…the mammoth is gone!" Bob regretfully announces. Dr. Charles rears his head back as he loses his smile and looks distraught.

"What?" a baffled Dr. Charles responds. Bob is nervously shaking his head as he looks at the costume halves, then gives Dr. Charles a pathetic look.

"It was the strangest thing. But right before I was locking up for the night, a young fella showed up and delivered a baby mammoth," Bob informs as he tosses the costume on the desk. Dr. Charles takes a double look as he picks up the costume and examines it. Then he flashes a curious expression.

"A baby mammoth?" Dr. Charles questions out loud. He takes a closer look. "Hmm…no eyes." Bob leans forward.

"Maybe they're born without eyes," Bob suggests. Dr.

Charles gives Bob a half grin.

"Bob, it's a costume," Dr. Charles responds as Bob sheepishly lowers his head, then he looks at Dr. Charles.

"I'm sorry, Dr. Charles…but I tried calling Dr. Freeman…I feel so bad, I thought I was doing the right things," Bob says as he lowers his head again in shame. A sympathetic Dr. Charles places his hand on Bob's shoulder.

"You were tricked, Bob. It's not your fault. The question is by who and why," Dr. Charles says as he suspiciously looks at the costume. "A mother would know her baby…unless she knew the culprits." He stares off, holding his chin between his thumb and a bent index finger while shaking his head.

"But that would be impossible, very strange," Dr. Charles mutters out loud.

"Well, it's a huge animal. I'm sure someone has spotted the beast," Bob says. Dr. Charles gives Bob a serious look.

"Look, make sure no other animals have escaped, and I'll call the police," Dr. Charles announces. Bob quickly walks away, leaving Dr. Charles with a puzzled look.

"Very strange," Dr. Charles mutters softly. "Very strange indeed."

The morning light continues to grow stronger as the boys steadily direct Big Mama down the drainage canal toward their destination: the desert. The drainage canal is lined with mesquite and Mexican palm trees near the residential side, while a fifteen-foot-tall sound barrier wall made of cement lines the interstate on the other side. All of this serves as good cover for the group. The boys pause for a second and share a smile with a nod, knowing that they have brought Big Mama successfully to the desert.

"We're almost there," JJ announces as the boys resume their walk.

Back at the golf course, the police officers are standing by a huge footprint that leads down the thirteenth fairway from the tee box. One of the officers leans his head to his mic clipped to the chest pocket.

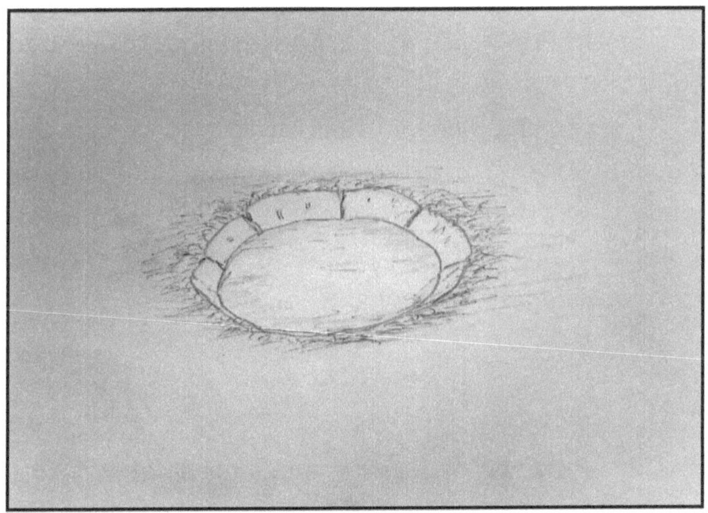

"Yeah, Chief, it looks like the subject is headed south. Over," the officer states. "And, Chief, this is a pretty big animal. This footprint is about two and a half feet by two feet. We might need backup."

Dr. Charles is sitting at his desk with one hand holding his chin in his customary fashion and the other hand's fingers tapping the desktop. His eyebrows are lowered, and his face is tense. Suddenly, the phone rings. He looks at the phone, then picks it up.

"Dr. Charles here, City Zoo…Hmm, south, interesting…Helicopter and a tranquilizer round, very good, Detective, thank you." He hangs up the phone. He looks despondent and puzzled as he lowers his head into his folded arms on the desk. Then he lifts his head slightly and sports a quizzical expression.

"There's something more here than meets the eye. Does somebody know something that nobody knows? Is this going to be a moment to behold, or is this going to be a moment we lose?" Dr. Charles softly says as his eyebrows lower, looking in deep thought.

It's later in the day as JJ peeks over a group of bushes. In the background Calvin and Brad are feeding Big Mama small branches of leaves. The group is gathered at the end of the canal that runs into the desert ravine. Because of its rainwater runoff, a healthy amount of mesquite trees and bushes flourish, serving as a great hiding area. Big Mama uses her snout and takes a branch of leaves from Brad.

"She's making me hungry," Brad announces.

"I bet her baby is hungry," Calvin says.

"We got company," JJ informs. "There's a couple of polices cars patrolling the area."

Suddenly, the wind slightly picks up and catches JJ's attention. He scans the area and sees the top of the Mexican palm tree blowing in the breeze.

Things are somber at the zoo as Dr. Charles quietly stands and blankly stares out the office window. He's perplexed at the circumstances surrounding the woolly mammoth but can't understand how and why things are happening. Suddenly, there's loud pounding on the door. He slowly turns his head toward the door, then slowly, as if dejected, turns his head back toward the window.

"Yes, come in," Dr. Charles mildly responds. The door quickly swings open, banging against the wall. Dr Freeman rushes through the doorway with his lab coat flapping and his arm moving wildly as he holds some papers.

"It's a miracle! It's impossible! I can't believe it, but it could only be a miracle!" a very enthusiastic Dr. Freeman says. Dr. Charles quickly turns around and flashes a questionable look at Dr. Freeman.

"Dr. Freeman, what is a miracle?" Dr. Charles asks as Dr. Freeman holds his head between his hands and rapidly paces the floor. He looks beside himself, then looks at Dr. Charles.

"Sir, the mammoth's antibodies can destroy the infected elephant's deadly virus. Dr. Charles, we have found a cure!" an elated Dr. Freeman announces.

Dr. Charles looks astonished, his eyes wide and his jaw dropped. He quickly walks over to Dr. Freeman, who is next to his desk.

"Dr. Freeman… are you sure about this?" an overwhelmed Dr. Charles asks.

"Yes, sir!" Dr. Freeman replies as he enthusiastically slams the research papers on the desk and gives Dr. Charles a joyful but serious look. Dr. Charles picks up the paper and sits down at his desk. His eye's tightly squint as he quickly reviews the lab results.

"Miracles are not impossible," Dr. Charles mutters to himself. Dr. Freeman looks down at the desk and sees the ragged costume but doesn't realize what it is. He looks at Dr. Charles.

"Dr. Charles," Dr. Freeman calls out. He looks up to Dr. Freeman.

"Yes, Dr. Freeman," Dr. Charles responds. The two men share a glance.

"Not only can we synthetically reproduce the antibodies serum, but the mammoth also recently had a baby!" Dr. Freeman announces as he picks up the fake baby mammoth costume and takes a double look. "Dr. Charles, this looks like a baby mammoth costume…with no eyes!" Dr. Freeman says with a chuckle.

Dr. Charles leans his back as his face gets tense. He slowly gets up from his desk and walks over to the window with a blank stare as he looks outside. Then he puts one hand on his hip and the other hand rubs his chin between his thumb and index finger.

"This is more than a miracle," an astonished Dr. Charles mutters to himself. He gives Dr. Freeman a serious look. "Dr. Freeman, the mammoth is gone. Bob was tricked last night by someone delivering a baby mammoth," Dr. Charles informs. Dr. Freeman sports a puzzled expression.

"Dr. Charles, how would anybody know this mammoth had a baby unless? Unless…they knew this animal ten thousand years ago," a perplexed Dr. Freeman states. "But that would be impossible, right, Dr. Charles?" The two men share a glance as if they both are realizing the same things at the same time, the total improbability of time travel.

"Dr. Freeman, time travel would be the only possible way for something so miraculous as this to happen. What great force took people to prehistoric Arizona for a reason and were involved in bringing back a species that went extinct nearly ten thousand years ago for only one purpose? Dr. Freeman, this wonderful animal is part of a greater story and is here today to give us a cure for a deadly disease to make sure its descendants do not end up being extinct like itself," an astonished Dr. Charles proclaims as Dr. Freeman gets drop-jawed at the thought; he is shaken and finds a seat.

"Time travel, we have lived to experience it," Dr. Freeman mutters out loud.

Chapter Twelve

BIG MAMA GOES HOME

Meanwhile, back at the ravine hiding spot, the three boys are next to Big Mama. The trees are swaying stronger, and the wind is starting to pick up the desert dust. Brad points to the sky at the sound of a thumping helicopter and gets wide-eyed.

"Look!" an excited Brad says as he points to the chopper. JJ and Calvin watch as the helicopter approaches their location, the thumping getting louder. But then the helicopter takes a tight bank and heads back in the direction it came from as the distinct thumping noise fades away. The boys share a smile of relief as they watch the helicopter fade out of sight.

"Sure, lot of activity in this area," Calvin comments as the wind steadily picks up.

"Dudes, the wind is really starting to get stronger," Brad remarks.

JJ crosses his fingers and closes his eyes. "Maybe, just maybe," JJ mutters to himself.

Surrounded by cement walls, trees, and bushes, the storm is out of view of the boys, but in the faint distance southern horizon, a dark wall of dust lines the landscape, above the line of dust, hazy blue skies.

In the sky a helicopter cockpit vibrates from the powerful engine that creates the loud thumping. The pilot, in his mid-thirties, is wearing his dark blue flight suit with dark aviator glasses. He adjusts the microphone mouthpiece that extends from his white helmet.

"Roger, we will head back south. Over," the pilot responds to an incoming message. He looks over to his copilot, who is holding a rifle with a scope.

"What's up?" the copilot asks as the pilot looks out the window.

"A bystander saw some kid with a large elephant cross the interstate this morning. We're heading back south," the pilot informs. "Did you bring any tranquilizer rounds?" he asks.

"Yeah, I'll load up," the copilot says as the pilot points out the window.

"Well then, we better hurry up. A storm is on its way,"

the pilot responds. The copilot pulls the bolt back to load the glass cartilage filled with the strongest dose of the tranquilizer available. Suddenly, the helicopter experiences a wave of turbulence, which causes an exceptional jolt to the aircraft. The copilot is caught off guard as he loses control of the tranquilizer round, and it falls to the floor of the craft. The copilot helplessly stares at the nonlethal munition as it rolls on the floor and out the side door, falling and smashing to the ground.

"Hey, we got a problem here!" the copilot desperately calls out to the pilot.

"What's up?" the pilot responds.

"We lost the sedative cartridge!" the copilot replies. The pilot nods.

"Then load a regular round and standby," the pilot informs the copilot. "I'll inform the command base." In a short moment of time, command has sent new orders. The pilot turns to the copilot.

"Orders are to proceed with a live round. Get ready!" the pilot instructs.

JJ is petting Big Mama's trunk, trying to keep her calm. Calvin and Brad are huddled near Big Mama's front legs. The surrounding trees and bushes are bending from the strong wind that has quickly ramped up. Dust and debris sail through the air as the small mesquite branches scatter throughout Big Mama's fur are starting to blow off. The boys can now see the massive wall of dust approaching fast as the wind starts to howl like a freight train.

"We're in luck. The storm is on its way. We got to get Big Mama out in the open desert. It's her only chance," JJ says. Brad points to the sky in the opposite direction of the storm.

"Look, they've come back!" Brad yells out as the sound of the approaching helicopter thumping quickly gets louder.

The boys gaze out in the direction of the helicopter with desperate faces.

"We better hurry!" Calvin says as he pulls his yellow handkerchief out from his backpack and wraps it around his face, covering his nose and mouth.

JJ walks up in front of Big Mama; he looks up at the frightened animal and pets her trunk, trying to keep her calm.

"I know you're scared Big Mama, but we're just trying to get you back to your baby," JJ explains. He grabs the rope tied to her tusk and starts to head toward the open desert. He turns around and looks up at Big Mama. "Follow me!" JJ commands as he leads the animal away from the canal ravine area and directly into the oncoming storm.

Calvin and Brad join JJ as the group struggles against the violent wind but know they must reach the desert flatland. The magical wall of dust is closing in; the wind, dust, and debris are making visibility difficult. JJ finds a good location and signals to stop.

"This should do it!" JJ yells above the howling wind. Suddenly, Brad frantically points toward the helicopter.

The helicopter quickly flies up above forty to fifty yards away and swings sideways. Then the side door swings open as the helicopter hovers in position. The copilot crouches down by the open door and starts to aggressively wave the boys to move with one hand while holding the rifle in the other, then he takes aim.

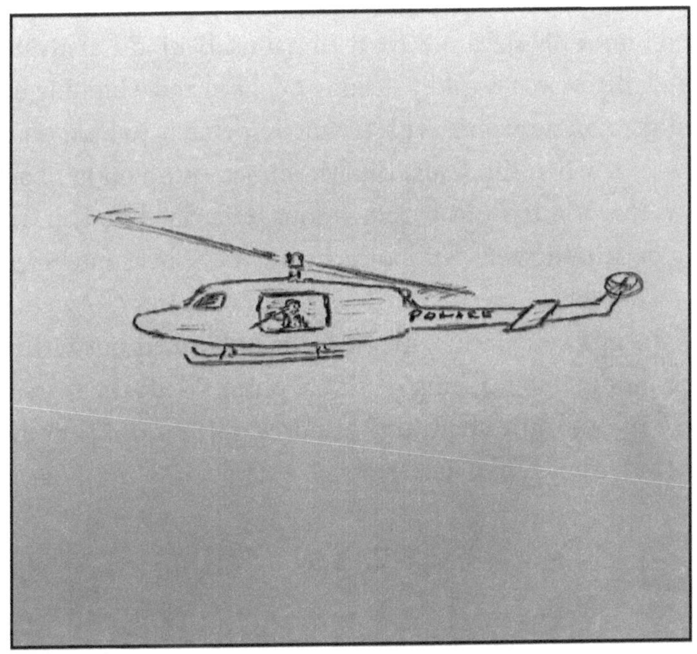

The boys are wide-eyed and fear for Big Mama as they look up toward the helicopter. They are taken by surprise that Big Mama is going be fired upon. To make matters worse, the howling and the constant thumping from the helicopter have taken its toll on the animal as she starts to get restless.

"Oh no!" Brad screams out.

"They're going to shoot her!" Calvin grabs Brad to get his attention.

"Come on, Brad, we got to try to stop them!" a desperate Calvin cries away. The two boys dash in front of Big Mama and frantically start to wave their hands. Behind Calvin and Brad, Big Mama is wildly shaking her head and whipping her trunk in all directions. JJ is trying desperately to hold on to the rope when suddenly, Big Mama stands up on her back two legs and lets out a tremendous roar. She lifts JJ in the air, creating a scene that looks chaotic to the helicopter crew.

"Woah!" JJ screams. Luckily, Big Mama's front legs return to the ground, along with JJ. He is unharmed but realizes the moment is reaching a critical point. With the massive wall of dust only about one hundred yards away, JJ knows the situation is now or never.

Up in the sky, the helicopter is struggling to keep its position in the intense wind. The copilot is kneeling in position with the weapon aimed at Big Mama. The pilot turns his head toward the copilot.

"It looks like the beast is out of control and a danger to the community. I can't wait for orders. Go ahead and shoot!" the pilot calls out. The copilot nods and tries to steady his arm as he takes aim.

"I'll fire a warning shot and get those kids out of the way" the copilot says.

Back at Dr. Charles's office, the phone starts to ring. Dr. Freeman, who is next to the desk, picks it up.

"Dr. Charles's office, Dr. Freeman speaking…I see. I'll let Dr. Charles know. Hold on, please," Dr. Freeman says as he pushes the Hold button and hangs up the phone. He walks toward Dr. Charles, who is blankly staring out the office window. He looks despondent and almost appears oblivious to the moment. Dr. Freeman walks up to Dr. Charles. He gives Dr. Charles a slumber look.

"Dr. Charles, the police need to know what you want to do. The situation is very fluid, and they have the mammoth in their sight. Dr. Charles, a tranquilizer shot is not an option, and they're saying the animal is a threat to the community, sir," Dr. Freeman respectfully tells Dr. Charles.

Dr. Charles's face cringes as his eyebrows lower, and he places his hand over his mouth.

"And death is an option?" Dr. Charles mutters to himself. "They just don't understand."

Meanwhile, back in the desert, things are tense. The wind is blowing violently, and the howling of the wind is deafening. The monster wall of the storm is only fifty yards away and closing fast. The two boys continue to desperately wave at the helicopter as they jump up and down. Calvin stops and turns to Brad.

"Brad, we have to take cover, or we might travel back in time with Big Mama!" an anxious Calvin cries out. Suddenly, a gunshot rings out, and the two boys get wide-eyed and share a glance.

"They're shooting! We got to get to JJ!" Brad yells out. The two boys dash up to JJ, who is struggling to keep Big Mama from total panic. The frightened animal is shaking her head and whipping her trunk in all directions. Calvin grabs JJ by the shoulder.

"Come on, JJ, we got to take cover! You need to leave Big Mama!" an eager Calvin says. The boys look out toward the storm, then share looks of panic.

"You guys better take cover!" JJ commands as the wall of dust is only thirty yards away. Brad gives JJ a determined look.

"You stay, we stay!" Brad proclaims.

Dr. Charles continues to stare out the window; he looks hopelessly disheartened. Dr. Freeman is anxiously standing next to him, then puts his hand on Dr. Charles's shoulder, who appears in the different world of thought.

"Dr. Charles, the police are waiting for your answer. Do they shoot?" Dr. Charles continues to look out the window, then gives Dr. Freeman a profound look.

"Dr. Freeman, this wasn't just a miracle. This was an intervention by some magnificent power. She has fulfilled her purpose," Dr. Charles states as he smiles at Dr. Freeman. "Let's find her a home." Dr. Freeman returns the smiles, then dashes over to the desk and picks up the phone.

"Don't shoot!" Dr. Freeman orders.

The pilot struggles to keep the helicopter in position as the copilot is set to fire any moment. Suddenly, the pilot turns his head.

"Roger. Over," he responds, then looks at the copilot. "Yo!" the pilot yells out loud as he waves his hand under his chin, signing to stop.

The boys are huddled together next to Big Mama's giant four legs. The storm is only ten yards away from engulfing the group. Suddenly, Calvin gets wide-eyed and points toward the helicopter.

"Look!" Calvin announces as the boys watch the helicopter turn around and fly away in the dusty sky. They share a smile.

"You guys take cover. I'll be right there," JJ informs. Calvin and Brad dash off as JJ walks in front of Big Mama and unties the rope. He looks up at the huge beast and sports a heartfelt smile.

"Maybe someday I'll know why we met. But it's time for you to go find your baby," JJ says as he gives her trunk a hug. "Goodbye, Big Mama." JJ sprints away toward Calvin and Brad as Big Mama lifts her huge head and lets out a mighty roar. Almost immediately, the massive wall of dust engulfs Big Mama like a giant tidal wave as she vanishes from sight.

JJ darts behind a large rock where Calvin and Brad have taken cover, instantly becoming engulfed by the storm as well. The wind is blowing violently, and the boys have vanished in the dust, but soon, the wind starts to ease up. The boys come back into view and are covered in dust. They share a curious glance and together stand up and look out toward the direction where they left Big Mama. The desert landscape is back to normal, but Big Mama is no longer present; the massive storm has taken her as the boys had planned.

CONCLUSION

The boys have blank faces as they stare out to where Big Mama was standing just a few minutes ago. They share the same thought and wonder if she made it back to her baby. Calvin gives JJ a somber look.

"Well, what do you think?" Calvin asks as JJ continues to stare off and shrugs.

"Destiny," JJ mutters out loud. Calvin and Brad give JJ a puzzled look.

"Destiny? What do you mean?" a curious Calvin asks as Brad looks on. JJ gives the two boys a somber look.

"Well, Inka talked about our destiny with the storm and how there's a reason for everything, I guess," JJ states as he gives Calvin and Brad a serious look. "But you know the bottom line?" JJ asks. Calvin and Brad give each other a baffled look. Then Calvin looks at JJ with a puzzled expression.

"What's that?" a curious Calvin asks. JJ looks at the two boys and smiles as he nods.

"We did the right thing, and that's all that matters," JJ replies.

"Dudes, I hope she got back to her baby," Brad says.

"Man, we'll never know," Calvin responds. JJ's eyebrows lower and his lips tighten.

"Like I said, we did the right things. And the rest was up to the Magical Storm," a melancholy JJ says as he nods and sports a soft smile.

"It'll be nice to know what happened," Calvin ponders out loud.

"Doing the right things was important, and I guess you don't always have to see the benefit," JJ says as Calvin nods.

"Or get a reward," Calvin adds.

"I did the right thing once," Brad proclaims. JJ and Calvin give Brad a curious look.

"Oh, what was that?" Calvin asks.

"I shared my lunch," Brad replies.

"How did you feel after that?" JJ asks.

"I was still hungry," Brad replies.

Calvin rolls his eyes while shaking his head as JJ lets out a chuckle.

"Hey, I almost forgot. My dad is taking me to the D-backs game, and we have a couple of extra tickets. You guys want to go?" an excited JJ asks.

"Yeah, a couple of hot dogs sound good!" Brad eagerly

responds. JJ looks at Calvin.

"How about you, Calvin?" JJ asks. Calvin flashes a suspicious look.

"Sure, if I don't have to sit next to Death Gas!" Calvin responds with a funny cringing face as the boys share a laugh and start to walk away.

The boys learned a valuable life lesson through their destiny with the Magical Storm: just do the right thing and let the outcome happen, whether you know it or not. They also realized that it's better to give than to receive and to always follow your heart.

A month later, Dr. Charles and Dr. Freeman's synthetical antivirus medication has been produced and successfully provided to the elephant kingdom, and almost like a miracle, the results have stopped the elephant extinction and have allowed the planet's largest mammals to freely roam their land. On top of Dr. Charles's desk, a newspaper lies with the headline that reads: "A Miracle, Elephant Saved."

Back in prehistoric Arizona, ten thousand years ago, give or take a couple of thousand years, Big Mama, and her baby strut away into the sunset. Their bodies are surrounded by the evening's dull orange glow of the sun, which is set against a bluish-orange sky. Big Mama lifts her head up high and lets out a thunderous roar as her baby watches her mighty mother. Together, the last mammoths fade away.

The End

MOTTOS TO LIVE BY

JJ says,
"Follow your heart!"

Calvin says,
"Strive to learn!"

Brad says,
"Play, make friends, and have fun!"

Visit *The Magical Storm* Collection
Merchandise available at
www.magicalstorms.com

9 798218 600426